RENT A BAE

AWAY TO AFRICA
BOOK ONE

UNOMA NWANKWOR

KEVSTEL PUBLICATION

KevStel Publications

info@kevstel.com

DEDICATION

Thankful to God from Whom the gift comes.

To Kevin, Fumnanya & Ugo

And finally, my readers. I love & appreciate you.

AUTHOR'S NOTE

Away to Africa is the second volume of my sweet romance collection, Afro Luv Bites.

Here, we follow the Kalu family. More specifically the three male cousins Arinze, Cheta & Jidenna. Rent A Bae is Arinze & Jasmine's story. We first meet them in New Year's Kiss which is a short prequel. Although you don't have to read that to enjoy this, I'd recommend it for maximum enjoyment.

Happy Reading!

In case you are wondering, the first volume, the Billionaire Pact is available on all major online retailers.

1

ARINZE KALU

I was supposed to find a wife, not have one forced on me.

I cleared the WhatsApp message from my grandmother and trotted down the stairs of my Atlanta home. I loved Mama, but recently her morning messages, which only used to consist of a prayer and Bible verse, now included some African proverb about marriage. Any other day, I'd respond to her immediately, but today wasn't gonna be that day. Strolling into the kitchen, I glanced at my watch. It was a quarter past six a.m.

I was late.

As a former Airman, I detested tardiness, but this morning, it couldn't be helped. My eyes roamed the granite countertop to locate my keys before my feet carried my tired body to the coffee machine in the corner. Relieved that my housekeeper had prepped it before she left last night, I started the machine. If I was going to have any chance of surviving the day, I needed to get some caffeine in me.

As I knew it would, my phone buzzed. I wanted to ignore Ciara, my assistant/secretary, but I knew she'd just call back.

Considering the significance of today and that I was already late, I didn't want to aggravate her further. With my Bluetooth in my ear, I connected the call.

"Please don't tell me you haven't left the house yet," she said, bypassing any kind of greeting.

I transferred the espresso into a travel mug sprucing it up to my liking. "Then I won't."

Picking up my keys, I headed out. I half listened to Ciara as she fussed about me not allowing her to hire a car service which would've gotten me out of the house already. As though they would've come and dragged me out of the bed. Before I could answer, she started to go down the litany of things I had to do for the day.

"Ci, you gotta let me breathe. It's too early." I interrupted her as the elevator to the underground garage opened.

She let out one of those dramatic sighs. "Nze, it's my job to make sure you're on point. Again, if you had let me do it, you wouldn't be driving yourself now."

"Noted!" I pulled on my beard.

It was as though all the women in my life recently came together and strategized on how to drive me insane. I needed a vacation, away from everyone. Since that wasn't going to happen in the next several months, I'd settle for tomorrow, Saturday, when I didn't have to do anything.

"Don't yell at me. You're about to make me go off on you, then you'll fire me—"

I grunted. "Let you tell it; I *almost* fire you every other week."

She feigned a few sniffles and I laughed at her silliness. "That should tell you how mean you can be."

I walked up to my G-Wagon and got in. The opening melodic chords of "Blinded by His Grace" by Stormzy floated through my speakers once I started the engine.

Ciara huffed. "Let me go talk to the producer in case you *are* late."

"Good deal." I pulled out of my parking space, and headed for the highway.

"Oh, get some caffeine in you. I need you in a better mood by the time you get here."

"Bye, Ci. See you in a bit." Without waiting for her response, I disconnected the call.

Ciara had been with me for two years and some change, and I couldn't remember what it was like before her. Sometimes though, I had to remind her that I was paying her and not the other way around. She was right; I was in a foul mood that needed to be put in check before I got to the television studio.

I considered myself a levelheaded man, but when I got tired, I got grumpy, and with that came the propensity to be easily irritated. It wasn't her fault that my connecting flight from Paris to New York had been delayed, causing me to miss my flight from New York to Atlanta. Instead of getting home yesterday morning, I made it in a few hours ago, throwing my entire schedule off.

As an actor, I was used to traveling, delays, and last-minute pivots I had to make; that was the least favorite part of my job. The silver lining in all of this was that the two-week European leg of press for my upcoming movie, *Blurred Vision,* was done.

Amidst the blare of horns due to construction going on at the ramp, I moved over to the express lane. I glanced at the dashboard to gauge how many minutes I'd be late. At this point it would probably be fifteen minutes. Today was the beginning of the US leg of the press tour. *Blurred Vision,* which would release in seven months, was my baby. In my fifteen years in Hollywood, it was my first faith-based film and one in which I acted in, and executive produced along with the studio.

Unlike my other movies, this was done by a mid-sized studio, so the plan was to get awareness out way ahead of time in order to help pre-sales. Even though I had a stake in the film's success, I also believed in its message, so I wasn't mad about doing my part to make sure it pulled in numbers.

Early flights, different hotels, and confusing time zones were all things that used to excite me once upon a time. As the years have gone by, I wanted my career to count for more than red carpets, talk shows, galas, and premier parties. As a first-generation Nigerian American, I couldn't have dreamed of the career I had. The expectation of me was to finish college and return to Nigeria to take my seat at Kalu International Inc. with my father and uncles. Somehow running the multimillion-dollar family business wasn't what I wanted to do. Exporting of spare motor parts, managing the car dealership and luxury bus line all seemed like the dream career when I was a kid, but that all changed after college. It was nothing but the grace and favor of God that was responsible for how my career had gone. Despite the fame and my bank account, I wanted to be a conduit for others like me to have an opportunity to achieve their dreams.

As a result of that drive, AKOne, my movie consultancy firm, was born a little over a year ago. Over the next five years, I wanted to transition to being more of a behind-the-scenes player. After all, that was where I started. My time in the Air Force opened a door to me being hired as a subject matter expert on mainly war or military combat movies. My job was to make sure that the language and behaviors of the characters that played fighter pilots were accurate and appropriate enough to give the film credibility. I liked it. It allowed me to use the experience I had in the Air Force to do something I have come to love. If there was ever a story about the steps of the righteous man being ordered by the Lord, it would be mine.

An hour later, I pulled into the reserved parking space for guests. Finishing the last of my beverage, I climbed out of the car. I removed my phone from my pocket and shot Ciara a quick text, letting her know I'd arrived. Following the instructions she gave previously, I jogged up the steps into the building. I greeted the receptionist and shortly after, a stocky man approached me.

"Good morning, Mr. Kalu. I'm Jed, the show's producer."

I shook his outstretched hand. "Good morning."

"Your assistant informed us that you might be late. Glad, it's only by a few minutes. If you'll follow me."

I nodded and fell in step as he tried to bring me up to speed on protocol. I'd done a million of these over the years, so I knew exactly what to do, but I understood it was his job to read me in. A few minutes later, I was in the makeup chair backstage, going through my messages with Ciara by my side. She clicked away on her trusted iPad while I responded to my grandmother, completely ignoring her marriage reference.

I messaged my mom, promising to call her later. The woman who knew she was my heart had a problem with me talking to my dad during my layover in Paris and not asking to speak to her. In her words, she couldn't believe her oldest and only son didn't ask to speak to her. I knew other Nigerian kids had to deal with things like polygamy and lack of any affection, but that wasn't my experience. Maybe it was because my parents attended Bowie State University in the sixties and had been influenced by American culture. My parents weren't typical Nigerian parents, my dad spoiled my mother any chance he got. She also knew she could get anything out of me. Except when she started singing the same tune my grandmother currently was.

With the important stuff out of the way, I journeyed over to Instagram. I had so many notifications and tags from my overseas tour. I liked as many comments as I could when the DM notification popped up. The decision to check it was a terrible one.

Chantel Morris.

The woman who'd single handedly tried to end my career and ruin my reputation. People always complained about men, but there was nothing worse than a manipulative and deceitful woman. Leaving her third message about still loving and missing me on "Read," I exited the app. Recalling the Bible verse my grandmother sent being about weapons forming against me not prospering, I said an "Amen." Whatever made Chantel remember me after five years, I needed the memory wiped ASAP.

I lifted my eyes from my phone as Jed walked back into the room. The cape was removed from my neck and Ciara did a quick inspection of my appearance. Since I didn't have any serious meetings today, I had on a light pink, cashmere sweater over dark, slim-fit cotton pants, finishing the look off with my white, red bottom sneakers. Nodding her head in approval, she took my phone from me.

"We're on a commercial break and you're on next," Jed said, as I followed him out. A few seconds later, he started his countdown, then the show was back on.

"Welcome back. Don't go anywhere. Next up, we'll watch live as Brianna and Cole, the winning couple from this season's *Unconditional Love* reality show, take their wedding vows," one of the hosts of *In the Morning* said.

"But first, the moment we've been building up to all week long. We finally have him in the studio. The winner of two NAACP awards, a BAFTA award, and an Emmy award nominee. He's starred in numerous chart topping movies, and recently, he branched into theater with the lead role in the adaptation of *Things Fall Apart* by the late Nigerian author, Chinua Achebe. But today, ladies and gentlemen, he's here for his upcoming movie, *Blurred Vision*. Please welcome to *In the Morning* none other than Arinze Kalu."

I rolled my shoulders and strolled onto the set amid the thunderous applause from the live audience. This never got old. Waving to the audience, I kissed both hosts on their cheeks and took my seat. The questions had already been provided, so I had an idea of what to expect. It was a nationally syndicated show, so I trusted they would stick to the script. There'd been a few times when, despite the agreement, I was asked questions about a past I so desperately wanted to forget.

"Thank you, ladies, for having me."

When another round of applause died down, the interview started.

"Your story always amazes me. From Atlanta, to Nigeria, back to Atlanta. College, the military to international movie star. Can you believe it?" Gia, one of the hosts, read from her cue card.

"Short answer, no." I chuckled. "Though born here, I grew up back home. At seventeen, I left Nigeria to attend Morehouse College, right here in Atlanta. After graduation, I was faced with the mandate to return home to join the family business. Although he didn't fuss, I knew that was my father's desire for me. I didn't know what I wanted to do, but I did know it wasn't that. I joined the US military instead. That experience changed my life."

"Who would've known that your time in the Air Force as a fighter pilot was the steppingstone for a career in Hollywood," the other host said.

"Yeah. After six years in the Air Force, I was no closer to figuring out what I wanted to do than I was at the beginning of my service. I went on a men's retreat with my church, and on the flight happened to be a Nate King—"

"The famous director, also known as the summer blockbuster King." Her eyes widened in awe.

"Yeah, we sparked up a conversation, but I didn't know who he was at the time. After the retreat, I got a call out of the blue. Next thing you know; I'm consulting for a war movie. That was all it was supposed to be. By some favor, I was in front of the camera some months later and fifteen years later, here I am."

"Here you are indeed. So, tell us about this movie, *Blurred Vision*, that opens in the fall.."

"Ah yes."

For the next couple of minutes, I told them a little bit about the movie. It was centered on a war prisoner who was given a new lease on life, but was having a hard time accepting it. The movie showed the main character's journey from viewing his future through the blurred vision of his past choices and trauma, to using God's clear lens and having the courage to aim higher. A clip was shown, of the part I played.

When we returned from a commercial break, a few more questions were asked and soon after, my microphone was being removed. I signed some autographs for the studio audience before making my way off the set. Ciara was waiting for me behind the cameras.

"Wassup, Ci?" I asked, taking my phone from her.

"Great job as usual. Glad you're in a better mood."

Ignoring her jab, I took the paper she was handing me as we made our way to the exit. "What's this?"

"It's the proposal Maria sent over for the writing gig. I know how you are about reading every single line, so I printed it out. You can read it as we ride to the next station."

"After that, what we got? I'm tired and hungry."

Her long nails clicked away on her iPad while her heels clacked against the marbled floors. "I can reschedule your meeting for noon, but you have two virtual interviews that can't be moved."

"With whom?"

"Damisi Danjuma of Mosaic Magazine and Olanma Rice of Limelight. We've moved them twice. They're going to print next week so we need to do this today."

I grunted. The Nigerian and South African publications had serious pull, and I didn't want to get on their bad side. I could do it from my home office, so it shouldn't be that bad.

She halted her steps and gave me a sour look. My eyes darted the area, before returning to her. I lifted a brow.

"Your girl keeps calling the office."

Annoyed, I continued on our path. Ciara was talking about Chantel and my instruction to her was the same.

She fell back in step. "Okay, I get it. I'll tell her you're not available. But I thought that after the fifth time, you'd want to see what she wanted."

"I don't. What else we got?"

"I also need the signed proposal for *Standoff 2*."

"I'll get it to you tonight." *Standoff 2* was a high budget major studio consultation I'd be handling, so I had to get on it.

As we neared my car, I saw Sean standing beside it. Sean was a college friend who served as my bodyguard. He had a security firm with a few guys, but he handled me personally. I didn't think I needed protection, but after the incident that changed my life some years ago and to give my mother peace of mind, I got with Sean. His burly frame towered over my 6'2" frame.

Getting closer to him, I threw my keys to him and gave him a dap. He and Ciara shared a church hug before she walked to her car, headed to the next destination.

"Hey man, I thought you were staying with the wifey today?" I asked. His wife, Dianne, had been discharged from a three-day stay in the hospital after a blood transfusion.

"She kicked me out. Said I was getting on her nerves. I hit Ci up and she said y'all were still here."

I chuckled at the sour look on his face. Sean was a few years older than me, and he and Dianne were my second example of long-term, Black couple goals—the first being my parents. Although the concept eluded me, seeing a couple with longevity and passion was a beautiful thing.

We climbed into the car, and he put the next stop in the GPS. As he pulled out, screeching tires caught our attention and a van flew by on two wheels. If not for Sean's quick reflexes, I was sure we would've collided with it.

"What the...?" I moved my attention away from my cousin Cheta's text just in time to witness the foolishness.

"That's what happens when folks don't leave their houses on

time," Sean fussed, leaning on the horn. The driver of the other vehicle waved his apology.

Bloom Floral Design.

I read the label on the van. I smirked as the memory from three months ago floated through my mind. Truth be told, the memory of a kiss with the florist at my boy's wedding, reappeared anytime I saw flowers.

Jasmine.

That's all she gave for a name. I wasn't a believer in the "there's only one true person for you" ideology. In my opinion, kismet was even more ridiculous. I believed in God. Was fate a thing? I felt so tethered to Jasmine that weekend, that I almost entertained the idea that destiny had brought us together.

Almost.

The way our lips collided while our tongues fought for control as we brought in the new year under the Jamaican skies was cosmic. After our lip lock, I planned to ensure we could explore whatever was between us. No matter how ridiculous it seemed. I left her under the gazebo to go get my jacket and tell my boys I was turning in. As I walked back to where she was, I *felt* her energy was off. I chided myself for the insane notion that I could *feel* her. Her back was turned towards me while she argued with someone on the phone. With the way she was carrying on, I knew it was a man.

That quickly cleared the euphoria I was in. No matter how beautiful she was—and she was gorgeous—never again would I deal with a woman with unfinished business. The last time it wasn't intentional, and I still paid a hefty price for it. I would be a fool to walk into another situation with my eyes wide open.

That was my cue to exit stage left. Mrs. Bisi Kalu raised a gentleman, so I wasn't going to leave her standing there without saying anything. When I made my presence known, she hurriedly disconnected the call. I walked her to her room and got myself on a plane back to Atlanta the next morning. I might not have been willing to engage with her any further, but that didn't mean she didn't leave an impression on me.

I leaned back in the seat and responded to Cheta. He and Jidenna were back in the city and our monthly meetup was overdue. Maybe we could put heads together and come up with a way to survive our impending Nigerian trip without coming back as married men to women we didn't even know.

2

JASMINE BOWMAN

I counted down in my head, trying to suppress the rage and sting of betrayal as I listened to this Betty White look alike try to sell me another pipe dream. Another yearly evaluation where Barbara Meadows, my boss at Bloom Floral Design, tried to sugarcoat the fact that once again, I wasn't going to get my promotion.

"Jasmine, once again, I have to commend you for the intricacy of design, excellence in installation and setup for the live wedding on the *In the Morning* show."

My expression remained aplomb as I struggled to keep my eyes from rolling. I'd been sitting in her office for twenty minutes as she repeated the same thing in a different way. It was Friday afternoon and I had one more design to put together for a wedding the next day. She knew exactly what she was doing with these repetitious compliments.

As assistant lead floral designer, I knew my work was good. I studied my craft and put my heart and soul into my creations. No matter what I did, or the extra work I took on because the lead designer, Amy, couldn't go a full week without calling out at least twice, it wasn't good enough. Case in point, the television show she was talking about. I was given only two days to prep because Amy suddenly had a family emergency.

Ten consecutive missed weekends and this woman was trying to play me. I kept reminding myself that I couldn't go to jail. If I cussed her out, I'd feed into the stereotype of the angry Black woman. Heck, I was angry.

"Thank you," I responded when it was apparent she needed a response.

For the next few minutes, she highlighted my opportunities for growth, development, and things I was currently doing well. When she was done, she began shuffling irrelevant papers in front of her as though she didn't know why I was still seated. To save both of us time, I decided to remind her.

"Barbara…" We went by first names at Bloom, which was just fine considering I was losing respect for people that failed to keep their word. "When I moved from Chicago and agreed to stay on with Bloom, I did so with the promise that after a probationary period filling in for the lead designer who resigned, that I'd be allowed to interview for the job."

I kept my gaze on the older woman who was now wringing her hands. Her discomfort wasn't my problem.

"I did the job and according to you, I did it well. It's been two years and I'm yet to hear anything about it."

I did hear, but I wanted her to tell me. Amy had decided she wanted to be a stay-at-home mother. Then two months ago, she comes waltzing her way back into the office. From the gossip around the studio, she didn't like being with her baby 24/7. I had absolutely no problem with that. My problem was that everyone seemed to forget that I was still owed the position they promised.

"Yes, I remember. As you know, things didn't work out as we planned." Her eyes darted to all corners of the office, deliberately avoiding mine.

My temples throbbed at the disrespect. This time around,

instead of nodding and giving her a way of escape, I kept my expression blank. Giving her enough rope to hang herself.

"You've done a phenomenal job and we don't want to lose you, so I've talked to Claudia and we're going to look for another role that will better suit your skills."

Leaving Chicago would never be a regret of mine. I needed to get away from that city. But when I put in my two weeks' notice, Claudia, my former boss, and owner of Bloom begged me to transfer to the Atlanta office. Bloom was one of the nation's largest floral companies. They specialized in high end engagements, weddings, and other events.

Flowers and the things that could be done with them was my passion. But working for such a huge company took all of my time. When I quit, the plan was to slow down for a while, since I didn't hate my job, I stayed on. It was the stringing me along that grated my nerves. I had no one to blame but myself. I was done with this discussion.

"I need to take a few days off." I needed a staycation to reevaluate my life.

"Uhm…oh, okay. The Blackwell wedding is—"

"Tomorrow, I know. I'll work the wedding, but I need some days after that." My raised brows dared her to deny my request. I stood and so did Barbara.

"Okay sure."

I muttered my thanks and made my way to the door. Barbara calling my name stopped me before I opened it.

"We really appreciate all your hard work at Bloom. We can't pay you enough."

Yeah, that was code for them knowing they were not paying me what I deserved. Once again, I willed my eyeballs to say in place. Hitting her with a head nod, I opened the door and walked to the bank of elevators of the five-story building. This top floor was where senior management sat.

I got in and pressed the button to take me two floors down to the design studio. The lobby was on the first floor, the consultation/showroom on the second, the storage and design studio on the third, then the sales team and other administrative staff occupied the fourth floor.

Stepping out of the elevator, I shuddered and drew my light cardigan over my shoulders. The chill from the flower storage coolers could be felt all the way from the hallway. The light pastel and white painted walls were adorned with pictures from various high-profiled, Atlanta weddings Bloom had done over the years.

I had four hours left in my shift and I had to complete the last piece of the Blackwell boho garden design. Everything needed to be ready to go in the morning. On my way to the cooler, I glanced at the floral recipe for the centerpiece. I needed some terracotta fancy carnations, baby eucalyptus greenery, and beige blush quicksand roses. The rest of my materials were already at my table. My phone buzzed in my back pocket. I pulled it out and stared at the notification.

Derrick: Babe, stuck in Chi town. I won't be able to make it this weekend. Call you later tonight.

I stared at the message and this time my eyes did roll. I promised myself a life reset at the beginning of the year. The day after New Year's to be precise. Here it was March, and I was still caught up in the same mess.

Thinking of New Year's Day had my mind going to the kiss that I thought for a tipsy second would change my life. What a disappointment that turned out to be, even before whatever it was started. I responded with a simple "OK" then went on about my business. Yep, I needed these next couple of days. If I didn't do something now, I'd be in this same rut come next year.

$\sim$

"Jazzy! Jazzy!"

It was barely eleven a.m. but since it was Wednesday and her day off, I knew my loud-mouthed bestie would be making her appearance soon. I pulled down another dress I hadn't worn in over a year and walked out of my closet. I threw the garment in the donation pile on my bed.

"In here," I yelled, bobbing my head to Ella Mai's "Leave You Alone." Me and my girl were having a moment with these lyrics.

Seconds later, Aubree Chapman entered my room and turned up her nose. I mirrored her expression, but I was sure it was for totally different reasons.

"Where is my god baby?" I asked.

My best friend was one of the baddest and smartest chicks I knew. Clad in a simple, white tee over faded ripped jeans that hugged her hips, she ignored me, as she headed to the laptop to turn off my music. I chuckled at her pettiness.

Aubree has been my best friend since the ninth grade. Some years ago, she and her now husband, Rich, relocated to Atlanta. He was a paid Black man in tech while she was an associate professor of chemistry at Spelman College. Even when we were miles apart, we shared everything, so now that we lived in the same city, I knew she wouldn't allow me more than a few days to be in my feelings. She lasted three days. That was a record.

"Bree, I was listening to that."

She was only a few weeks older than me, but swore she was my mama.

"Ali is with her daddy. You, on the other hand, need a coming to Jesus." She tucked one of the passion twists back in the bun on top of her head and plopped down on the sofa near my bay window. "I gave you three days, now I need to get you all the way together."

Shaking my head, I grinned and walked back into my closet. Any time I retreated, she got so bothered. I loved her so much, but after all this time, she still didn't understand that sometimes I just needed to be.

"We already know Jesus." I reentered the room with a pair of shoes I'd worn only once.

"Hmmm. If you did, you wouldn't be over here bonding with Ella Mai on how y'all can't leave no good men alone. Instead, you'd let James Bay talk some sense into you."

My brows came together at her reference to the 2015 song titled, "Let it Go." I cackled. "No, you didn't go way back."

Aubree folded her leg under her. "Girl, don't play. You know that was the jam that stayed on repeat when we were in our feelings."

I shook my head at the memory of our yesteryears.

Aubree picked up her phone. "Let me check on Rich and my baby, then we'll tackle your crisis."

I got back to my spring purge. Not waking up to an alarm that morning was heaven. The free time gave me a lot of time for reflection, and I was unhappy with what looked back at me. That unhappiness led me to start purging old stuff out of my closet. There was a lot of old stuff I needed to purge out of my life, but at least this was a start.

The babble of my goddaughter pushed my thoughts to the background. I scurried back into the room.

"Hey auntie's god baby," I cooed, taking the phone from Aubree.

My voice got an excited spew of gibberish from Alicia. She was strapped to her daddy's chest while he pushed her stroller through Centennial Olympic Park. After I had gotten my fill of her cuteness, I greeted her father.

"Wassup, Jazzy? Thought you didn't see me."

"I did, but the queen comes first."

The three of us shared a laugh. I was in the room when that baby was born. Since the day she graced this earth with her presence, she'd captured my heart.

"You left that loser yet?" Rich asked, completely taking me by surprise.

I cut my eyes at Aubree, and she shrugged. It was no secret they couldn't stand Derrick, but Rich did a pretty good job of not saying much. So, this was all Bree.

"Don't look at her. He's a punk. I told you I got someone for you. But I'm not trying to be in the middle of anything. So, when you're completely over D, let me know."

Before I could respond, Aubree chimed in.

"Don't worry babe, I'm about to get her together. Take care of my baby. I love you."

"Woman, I got this. Love you too. Y'all be good."

After blowing each other air kisses, the couple disconnected the call.

"Aww look at you two—Black love. It's giving, and I love to see it." I walked back into the closet.

"And I'd love for you to have it. But you can't seem to let go of D's trifling behind."

I peeked back out of the closet, and she pulled out her iPad. I wondered what she was up to, but couldn't ponder on it that long because my phone started ringing. Before I could walk to the dresser to pick it up, Aubree had it in her hand.

"Ugh, please let him roll over to voicemail." She rolled her eyes and handed me the phone.

I did send Derrick to voicemail, but not because she asked me to. Like I said, I'd been thinking. Last weekend was the third time he'd been "stuck" in Chicago. Then had the nerve to not even call me until just now. I really had nothing for him. After ringing a couple of times, he sent me a text, presuming I was busy with a client, so he'd hit me up later.

The heat of Aubree's stare caused me to turn around. "What, Bree?"

She let out a long, exaggerated breath. "You know I see through all that puffing you're doing." She tapped the space next to her. "Sit down, Jasmine. We purged that closet two weeks ago, remember?"

She wasn't lying. Whether I wanted to or not, we were about to talk, so why not get it over with. Acquiescing, I replaced the empty hanger, and walked into my bathroom to wash my hands. After drying and moisturizing them, I took a seat next to her.

"I promise after this I won't talk about this again. I'll stick by whatever you decide."

I opened my mouth to speak, but she squeezed my thigh to silence me.

"Please let me get this out. We're both only children of our parents. I guess that's part of the reason we've stuck together like two dried figs. Blood sisters couldn't be any closer. We've been together through everything. Your parents' sudden death, my grandmother's passing, my father's stay and release from prison. My trouble reconnecting with him and how I transferred that unresolved trauma to Rich."

My eyes misted as she ran down the trials and victories we'd been through over the years. It'd been a decade since my parents died in a plane crash. The grief of that tragedy and the guilt of surviving nearly sent me under. I was supposed to be on that trip, but I was being bratty as usual and didn't go. The only family I had on this earth was my dad's sister, Aunty Delia, and her husband, George. Nothing could fill the void of losing my parents.

"After college in Cali, you wanted to move to Chicago. We did it together. My point is… I love you to pieces. When you hurt, so do I. What kind of sister would I be if I keep letting you go through life living beneath your potential?"

She sighed. "I'm just going to say it. That friends-to-lovers mess is the biggest scam in history. I get it, y'all grew up together. His pops and yours did business together. He's familiar, but you gotta let that go." She flailed her arms in the air. "One drunken night, y'all had sex and he's suddenly in love. Then two years in, he dares to break up with you via text? On New Year's Eve at that—"

"I get it, Bree. I was there, remember?" Her recalling that night strangely didn't have me angry at Derrick. Instead, it had me upset with the stranger I'd danced with that night.

"I don't think you do. Because letting him weasel his way back in a few weeks later, after he claimed to be drunk and mad at you cancelling y'all plans wasn't the move, sis. If I thought you loved him, I still wouldn't get it, but I'd respect it. But I know for a fact you don't."

I rolled my eyes. "Don't act like you know me."

She giggled. "But I do. The only reason you're still with him is you're so afraid to love and lose again."

I stood, but she grabbed my hand. "Like you lost your parents and Eddie. You're willing to settle for Derrick because there's no risk in being with him."

The ache from the mention of Eddie was still there, although it was a dull one. My first real love that crashed under the weight of my grief. He didn't know how to help me, so helped himself to the blondie in the apartment next to mine. Their wedding announcement was why I ended up with Derrick and in this rut I was currently in.

"Don't do that," Aubree said, sensing my melancholy. "If that man fell into another woman—white, Black or purple—simply because he couldn't snap you out of your grief, he wasn't yours in the first place."

"You're right. I don't love Derrick, but I do care about him a lot."

"That's not enough reason for you to let him treat you like an afterthought."

"He's under a lot of—"

"Please Jas, he got a job here a year ago and refused to move, giving every excuse in the book. Then he blames you for your schedules not syncing to manage a long-distance relationship."

"I agree. But Derrick isn't my problem right now. My job is..."

"I'm getting to that, but you have to get rid of dead weight to elevate. Light skinned and fine, I wouldn't put it past him to have confiscated your destiny."

I flung my head back as laughter ripped from the pit of my stomach. She joined me. Her dad was light skinned and she transferred all her issues with him to every light skinned, Black man she came across. I was glad Rich was a dark roast brother because her indecisive behind gave him enough problems as it was.

"Now that's a stretch. This Ted Talk of yours has me starving. The chicken should be well marinated by now."

Aubree sprung to her feet. "Girl, yes. What are you making?"

"Your favorite." Picking up my phone, I headed out of the room. "I knew your nosy behind would be here today, so we're having French onion chicken."

Aubree squealed, picked up her iPad and followed me.

"You're mighty close to that iPad today. Wassup?" I pulled out the frying pan and chopped up some onions.

Ignoring my question, she pulled out a barstool and made herself comfortable. "I figure you don't need my help."

I waved her off. Neither of us loved to cook; however, when I did, I preferred to work alone. I loved my kitchen, but it wasn't big enough for both of us to be moving around in here. I spent long hours on Pinterest picking up design ideas. The dark tone with a contrasting light tone gave my galley style kitchen an airy feel. I finished off the modern style with cool furnishings and live plants.

As I busied myself preparing our meal, Aubree shared some stories about her students, Rich's sister, who she couldn't stand, and Alicia's upcoming birthday party. My god baby was turning two and I already had the floral arrangements and décor sketched out. Missing the first one because of work still made me so angry.

"Speaking of Bloom…"

I lifted my eyes. "We weren't speaking of Bloom." No way she could read my thoughts.

She rolled her eyes. "Anyway, you've always complained about being overworked, underpaid, and taken for granted. So, we're about to fix that too."

I turned on the oven to preheat. "Bree, did you wake up with me on your mind today? You're in all my business."

"And you'd be in mine if the situation was reversed."

She was right, so I let her continue on her soapbox while I filled a pot with water to steam the rice.

"If you're going to do all this work, why not do it for yourself? Being in business isn't for everyone, but you...you've always wanted your own flower shop. Remember Luxe Petals? I still have the logo we designed way back when."

I threw my head back and let out a breath. "Bree, opening a flower shop requires money. Big money, a great location, staff, a van for deliveries..."

Aubree listened as I continued to enumerate all the things that stood in my way. I majored in business, but my passion was in design and flowers. During grief therapy, I was encouraged to channel my creative energy into something I loved. I took some basic courses, quit my desk job in California and moved to Chicago to work for Bloom.

"Okay I hear you, but nowhere in your litany did you say you no longer want to own your own shop."

"Because I do."

"Then why don't you?"

"Haven't you been listening?"

Aubree smiled and opened her iPad. After typing an address in the browser, she turned it toward me. "Boom!"

Plating the sautéed asparagus, I squinted at the screen. I frowned, then turned my eyes to Aubree. "Rent A Bae. What the...?"

"It's the answer to our...well, your...no, our problem."

I scoffed. "You want to *rent* me out?"

She raised her hand in surrender. "I see you're ready to tussle, but hear me out."

"No! In fact, you're about to take this food to go. Maybe on the way you can find your mind because I'm sure you've lost it." Shaking my head, I continued what I was doing.

In true Aubree overbearing fashion, she couldn't take the hint. Instead, she started rattling something about the best way to break free from Derrick was to occupy myself dating someone else. Then she quickly clarified that it wouldn't even be considered a real date as I'd only be pretending to be the person's girlfriend, fiancée, or wife. According to her, the company had been in business for several years with thousands of stellar reviews.

I ignored her, yet to see how this idea would benefit me in any way. I didn't need to be rented out to get rid of Derrick. When she said I could be paid up to two hundred and fifty thousand dollars, I paused cutting up the garnishing and slowly turned to face her.

"Really, Jazzy? A knife?"

I looked at the utensil in my hand. "Girl, ain't nobody trying to stab you." I pointed the knife toward the iPad. "Two-Fifty K, for a make-believe date. What's the catch?"

Her brows came together, and she bit her lower lip.

I placed my free hand on my hip. "Bree!"

"They do top notch background checks and—"

"Aubree!"

She placed her hand over her eyes and rattled so fast I almost missed it. "International travel will most likely be required."

I chuckled in disbelief. I watched the *Tinder Swindler* on Netflix last night and here my friend was suggesting signing up to possibly star in a show of my own.

3

ARINZE

heta laughed, lifting his head from the mini fridge. "Nze, you can't do that!"

I shifted my focus from the cue ball and stood with the cue stick. Blowing out a frustrated breath, I frowned at him. "Why not?"

He swaggered over to me, lifting a Malta bottle to his lips. He patted my shoulder and leaned against the billiard table. He was the jokester out of the three of us, but nothing about what I'd been going through the past week was funny.

The culprit? My grandmother.

Last New Year's Eve, she somehow convinced my grandfather to sit with her while she threatened I and my two cousins to find wives before she did it for us. I, and my cousins, Cheta and Jidenna, were the grandsons of the Kalu family. Let my grandmother tell it, our continued bachelorhood was threatening the family name.

"My husband's bloodline will not end with the three of you. Get married—you refuse. You're not getting any younger. Okay, I'll find women for you," she'd threatened.

At that time, I ignored her fuss. She wasn't in America, so

24

what harm could she do? Now, my sister decided to move her wedding up, so we were headed to Nigeria in two months. My grandmother cranked up her harassment last week. I had too much going on and could do without her incessant calls narrating her dreams of and prayers for my "wife." I loved talking to her, but recently, it had become a chore. I hated it. I'd just filled Cheta in on my plans to tell my grandmother flat out she needed to stop it, or I'd stop answering her calls.

Despite our best efforts, my cousins and I weren't able to get together last weekend. We attended church this morning and they all followed me to my house afterwards. Since we attended first service, we were out in no time. I cooked breakfast, something I'd been doing since the three of us shared an off-campus apartment when we attended Morehouse. Being three and four years older than Cheta and Jidenna respectively, I was a senior by the time they joined me in America.

"You can't tell Mama no. Or rather, I don't want to be there for the aftermath."

Cheta set the bottle down on the side table. I stared at him, waiting for him to make his point. As the oldest, I was getting the brunt of her harassment, but they weren't in the clear, so we needed to present a united front when we saw her. How age equated to the need to be married was still a mystery to me.

"I still don't understand your point."

"What point?" Jidenna reentered the room after taking my niece, his six-year-old daughter, Uju to her room. My niece lived with her father, but had a room set up in my and Cheta's homes. After her mother passed away, the three of us raised her together. She was the center of our world.

"Nze wants to tell Mama to stay out of his business," Cheta exaggerated. We all loved our grandmother, but he was a big softie when it came to her.

A scowl appeared on Jidenna's face. "You want to tell her...what?"

I waved him off. His case was far different. He'd been married right out of college. So, the family kinda tiptoed around him. If only they knew him like Cheta and I did. Jidenna was quiet, but fragile was something he wasn't.

"Our problem is we don't set boundaries," I started, hardly believing the crap I was saying. The blank stare from my cousins caused me to burst out in laughter and they joined in.

When we gathered ourselves, Jidenna spoke, "Man please, we grew up here and I'm so thankful for the opportunity, but you know that doesn't fly back home." He picked up his cue stick. "They think they are entitled to our business."

"I know, but that doesn't make it right. We should be able to set boundaries without feeling guilty." I placed the cue ball in position.

Cheta shook his head. "I get that. We're grown, but ask yourself if it's worth it in this case. Mama is old old… are you really trying to argue with her?"

Jidenna nodded. "Avoiding her is not the answer either. We'll be in Nigeria for two weeks." He shrugged. "I mean, you can run to Ibadan to be with your mom's side of the family, but you know your sister will be hurt. It's her wedding after all."

I sighed as I simmered on the truth of what they were saying. I could tell my grandmother no, but was it worth all the *wahala?* I had to look for a way to appease her for the time I was there. When I returned, the luxury of rushing her off the phone could return. No matter how much I wanted to appease her, having her force a woman on me while I was there wasn't an option I'd condone.

Unlike my uncles, Cheta and Jidenna's fathers, who had Igbo wives, my dad married a Yoruba woman. Her family lived in the western part of Nigeria. Hiding out there wasn't an option either. For the reason Jidenna mentioned and also, I was no longer the rebellious teenager who needed his very chill, rich Yoruba uncle to intercede on his behalf.

"What time does the game come on?" Cheta's voice broke through the riot going on in my mind. He picked up the remote and flipped through the channels on the large flat screen mounted on the wall.

"What game?" I asked.

"Georgia State...NCAA."

Jidenna and I looked up at him. He was drafted into the NBA right out of college and after a stint with two other teams, he was now a point guard for the Atlanta Harriers. They failed to qualify for the Eastern Championship by three points. Something he blamed himself for. So, for him to be looking to watch any basketball game, even college, surprised us. After responding that we weren't sure, Jidenna and I shared another look and went back to playing billiards.

We temporarily shifted from talking about our impending trip back home to what we had going on in the next couple of months. Since his season was over, Cheta would be fulfilling his usual contractual obligations with his various brands before we left. While Jidenna and I would head back to the States right after the wedding, Cheta was planning on chilling out in Naija for a while. He'd spend time with his parents and at the same time, oversee Tune Up. The three of us opened a male grooming salon in Enugu, our hometown, and were building another in Lagos.

Jidenna, who was a sculptor, had a show coming up in Paris, and then Johannesburg in the coming months, while it was back to work for me. During our conversation, the doorbell rang. It was Door Dash. While Jidenna went to answer, I left Cheta shouting and cursing at the television while I ran up the stairs. I checked in on my sleeping niece. Minutes later, I walked back in on my cousins already eating.

"You guys couldn't even wait?"

"Not when *isi ewu* is concerned," Cheta responded while Jidenna chuckled.

We'd ordered from the number one Nigerian restaurant in

Atlanta. Drawing the corner stool closer to me, I opened the container they'd left for me. The aroma of coconut rice and spicy snails wafted up my nostrils. I bowed my head, gave thanks, and dug in.

"Got it!"

I almost spit out the rice I'd just put in my mouth.

"*O we ife ne me gi nisi?*" I asked if he was crazy in our native tongue.

"No. But you will thank me when I tell you I have the solution to your problem."

"And you couldn't just say that?" Jidenna asked.

I agreed, but now wasn't the time to debate it. I needed to hear his idea. "Wassup?"

"As I was watching the game, I saw that stupid Vance sitting courtside."

I decided not to engage my cousin as the venom he had for his former teammate and franchise player for Philadelphia rose to the surface.

"No amount of insult can change the past. Stop letting him take up unnecessary space in your head. What's the solution to Nze's problem?" Jidenna voiced my thoughts.

"I remember years ago when we went to the wedding of one of his homies—one real estate broker. Folks were whispering that he met his wife through a service—"

"I'm not in the market for a wife." I quickly corrected him.

"Nze, chill out. It isn't a match making service. It's where you can rent a person to pretend to be whatever you need them to be. Girlfriend, fiancée, or wife. Same goes for boyfriend etc."

I laughed out loud. Like head back and pepper almost going to my brain laugh. "You want me to rent a human being?"

"Rent A Bae."

"Huh?"

"You would be renting a bae." Cheta gestured with his hands

as though I was stupid for not catching on. "That's the company's name," he clarified.

Jidenna glanced at Cheta then his eyes landed on me. He seemed to be as skeptical as I was. I was really still stuck on renting someone. I knew all about match making services, but those people were looking for a love match. I wasn't. Furthermore, my need was for international travel. I guess I didn't answer quick enough for Cheta because he shrugged, took the volume of the television off mute, and returned to his food.

Jidenna turned to me. "Bros, the wedding is two months away. It's either you find a girl to get serious with—"

"I don't have time for that—" I quickly shut that down.

"Then get ready to entertain the person Mama has waiting—"

"Not an option."

Jidenna shook his head and chuckled. "Cheta, get the contact info of the company. Let's see wassup first."

The food in front of me suddenly lost its taste.

Two weeks later, I swatted an unwanted bee that buzzed too close to my ear. The pollen wasn't too bad for a mid-spring day, but I had no desire to be outside any longer. I performed a mental run down of the things I had to do before returning to the office. I was grateful to Ci for saving me from my niece's wrath. I was all set to make a quick run to Detroit when she reminded me of my niece's recital this afternoon. It was now over, and I was leaned against my truck, waiting on her father to finish talking to the dance instructor. The dance studio was located in a Black-owned shopping complex.

As I absentmindedly scrolled through my phone, I caught Cheta who had been on the phone, stalking back over to where I was. I could see the stress lines etched on his forehead. He leaned against the truck and grunted. He had been on the phone arguing with his management team.

"*Ke kwanu?*"

"I dey. Who were you screaming at?" I asked.

His brows came together in a frown, causing me to chuckle. "Don't play me. I don't scream. I shout."

This was why I couldn't take him seriously. "Whatever you were doing, what's the problem now?"

My phone dinged in my hand, and I saw I had a message from my sister.

"Are you minding…"

I looked up from my phone because his voice trailed off. Following his line of sight, I shook my head. The lady he was admiring was beautiful. At least from the part of her I could see. She had short blonde hair that complimented her milk chocolate skin.

I looked back over at Cheta. "Put your tongue back in your mouth. You already have unfinished business. Adding a woman to the mix right now is not the way."

We both dressed down so didn't fear drawing any attention our way. Cheta pulled down his ball cap and waved me off. "It might not be the way…" He growled and nodded in approval of the woman. "But that doesn't mean I don't want to move in that direction."

"Well don't."

Remembering the message, I received seconds prior, I looked down at my phone. My sister had sent me a video with a couple of laughing emojis. I made a mental note to call her. For an impending bride, she was surprisingly calm. When Cheta's older sister got married, I remembered her calling me often. As the oldest grandchild that the folks would listen to, she needed me to talk to the extended family about their outrageous demand for the traditional rites. If any man wanted my cousins, they had to do what was necessary, but I was opposed to exploitation because there was an opportunity.

I clicked on the video and heard my grandmother's voice. That caught Cheta's attention, so he leaned closer. We watched as my grandmother came into focus, twirling some lady around. She hyped the lady in our language while the young woman acted all shy. My brows came together in confusion. I wondered why my sister sent this to me until my grandmother spoke again. With wide eyes, I watched while my heart raced as rage poured through my body.

"My grandson, Arinze will love you. *Asa m! Chai, ne go du! Omalicha nwa.*"

The woman, who looked to be in her twenties, smiled sheepishly and strutted a short distance as though she was in a beauty pageant. My grandmother clapped. From the way the camera was positioned, I knew that whoever was filming wasn't supposed to be there.

My grandmother continued, "See those childbearing hips and full breasts for feeding my great-grandchildren. Welcome my daughter. Keep yourself pure o! Arinze will be here soon for my granddaughter's wedding." My grandmother snapped her fingers and folded her arms across her chest as though she was in awe. "Your grandmother said you were beautiful, but I didn't expect this level of beauty..."

The video ended mid-sentence and I was stunned mute. I wasn't sure what made me angrier. My grandmother's audacity or Cheta who was bent over in a fit of laughter. From my peripheral, I saw Jidenna and Uju approach. Cheta was still laughing when he picked up Uju.

"Wassup?" Jidenna asked.

Cheta continued to laugh.

"Man, shut up. It's not that funny." I nudged him

"I know you lying. That mess is hilarious." Cheta took the phone from me and gave it to Jidenna.

"Uncle Cheta are you laughing at my video? Did you record it?" Uju turned her head to her dad. "Daddy, let me see."

Cheta tried to control his laughter and shook his head. "I did film you, Ju. You were great." He kissed her cheek and she giggled. "We'll watch you on the big TV in my house. I'm laughing at Uncle Arinze."

I felt her eyes on me as I watched for her father's reaction. His face was blank, so I met my niece's stare. "Wassup, Beautiful? You were fantastic today."

"Why is Uncle C laughing at you? That's not nice."

She balled her face up in a frown and I kissed her cheek. "That's because your Uncle C is silly. Are you ready for ice cream?"

Cheta opened the door of my truck, put Uju in, then made sure she was secure. He gave her an iPad to keep her entertained before closing the door. Jidenna walked over and handed me the phone without saying anything. He seemed fine earlier, but the solemn look on his face had me wondering how he was doing. He'd gotten a lot better over the years, but the grief of Uju's mom's death crept up at any given time. Cheta and I stared on as Jidenna walked to the other side to get in the back with his daughter.

"No comment?" I asked.

He shrugged his shoulders. "At least she's pure." He grinned and got in the backseat.

Cheta and I burst out in laughter. It was funny, but it really wasn't.

"Aye," I called out to Cheta. "*Abeg*, fast, fast, hook up that Rent A Bae thing for me. I see your grandmother is serious." He had free time and I had to go out of town on a promo duty.

Cheta laughed. "Okay, should take about a week or two."

"*Daalu*." I threw the keys at him. "Drive. Let me call my mom and figure out what's going on." We got in the car and Cheta pulled out of the complex.

"Aunty B will be sleeping. Let her be," Cheta said.

"She's not in Enugu. She's in Canada with Adaugo for last minute wedding stuff." I dialed.

"*Omo mi.* How are you doing?" my mom asked as soon as the call connected. She always called me "my child" in Yoruba. I greeted her and was about to ask for my sister when Cheta shouted.

"Aunty B! Good afternoon, ma."

"Is that my basketball star? Cheta, how are you?"

"Aunty, good afternoon, ma," Jidenna greeted.

We were a very close-knit family, so I wasn't surprised they wanted to say hi. My mom was well respected as the leader of the pack so to say. My dad was the oldest Kalu son. I didn't hear Uju, so I looked back to find her slouched in slumber.

"Mummy, wait. They'll call you on their own time. Where is Adaugo?"

"She's in the kitchen. Kayode, what's wrong?" she asked, calling me by my Yoruba name.

"Did she show you that video? What's your mother-in-law up to?"

My mom laughed and soon after, Adaugo came to the phone. "Brother, Ifunanya sent it to me. Apparently, she went to see mama who had a visitor." Ifunanya was my youngest sister. She just finished her master's degree in London and returned home to work for the family.

"*Omo mi.* There's no harm in entertaining her. You might like the young lady. I have been telling you it's time to settle down as well."

"But not like—"

My speech was cut short when Jidenna tapped my shoulder. I glanced at Cheta who shook his head also. I read their signals to stop talking about it. Agreeing, I changed the topic to the wedding plans. A few minutes later, I told them I loved them and disconnected the phone.

"Nze, no matter how you say it, you can't change their minds," Jidenna said.

"So, just trick their minds," Cheta added.

I leaned back in my seat. I grimaced at the slight chance that I may not have had to go through this if Ms. Florist was single as I thought she was. Anyway, I was now readier than ever to meet this person who would be my fake bae. There was no way I was letting my grandmother have her way. Not this time.

4

JASMINE

This was all Aubree's fault.

My focus lingered on the flickering flame of the candle that illuminated the otherwise dark room. After another morning of waking up way before my alarm was supposed to go off, I treaded to the bathroom, handled my hygiene, and lit the pink fig and spruce scent. I placed it on my dresser before sliding back between my sheets. I was counting on its calming effect. As with so many mornings before it, I knew slumber was over.

I rubbed my forehead and closed my eyes, letting out a deep sigh. I lived in Duluth, one of the northern suburbs of Georgia, so I couldn't blame my sleep issues on the thriving nightlife that downtown Atlanta boasted of. For the past week, my sleep had been choppy at best, and yes, I blamed Aubree.

My life was okay, not the best, but okay. I had a plan. I was going to take baby steps. Block Derrick's number, return to Bloom, but fix up my resume on LinkedIn. Get myself back in the job market. Her sermon of a week ago now made me a permanent resident of "overthinkersville." Possibilities I had long pushed to the recesses of my mind now played in a loop every day. Now she had opened that box, and I had a hard time closing it.

Pulling myself into a sitting position, I leaned against the headboard and secured my bonnet. I leaned over and pulled my laptop and notebook closer. Sliding my fingers across the mousepad, I woke the device up. 4.49 a.m. The site I had open last night before I drifted off stared me in the face.

Rent A Bae: We Take the Pressure Off.

I was still stunned something like this existed. The name was laughable, but apparently, there was a real need for their unique services. The website held little or no information about the process itself. There was a contact form where you'd have to request information. However, the reviews Aubree talked about were all stellar. The pictures showed exotic places all over the African continent. There were a few of some in Europe and Asia as well.

The owner was a widow, Mariam Appiah. She was Black American, and her late husband was Ghanaian. There was an exclusivity behind the service because I couldn't find a lot of interviews she'd given. In fact, I found only one on YouTube. I clicked on the second tab I had opened and pressed play on the video.

"I was married to my husband for thirty-five years before he passed. We were in the same history class. Our eyes met and it was magic. That doesn't mean we didn't go through our own share of problems. I'd heard so many stories about foreigners using us Americans for the benefit of a permanent status in the United States. So, at first, I gave him a hard time. Also, I had been told Africans don't like us. But I think we had to write a paper together. Yeah, I think that was it. I couldn't avoid my Kwasi any longer. In working together, when we began to listen to each other and understand that our experiences might be different, but we shared the same trauma from those who oppressed us. We became patient and kinder toward one another."

She laughed. "That man didn't want anything from me. He wanted to finish his degree and go back home to Ghana. There are people with bad intentions, but not everyone."

The interviewer asked her why she started Rent A Bae. Mrs. Appiah and her husband made their home in Ghana and New York. She talked about how her sisters-in-law always talked about the pressure of settling down.

"I used to feel so bad for them. As Black Americans, we have that pressure too, but in Africa, it's a whole thing. I say Africa because I also have friends from other countries in Africa and it's the same."

I got what she was saying. What my parents didn't live long enough to do, Aunty Delia did for them. Under the guise of wanting me to be happy and settled.

Happy…

When I was in active therapy, I remember my therapist asking if I was happy or distracted from sadness. Over the years, I'd ruminated over that question without coming up with an answer. I tuned back into Mrs. Appiah's interview when she mentioned changing the name to appeal to a wider age group on a nudge from her daughter. She'd seen an interview a billionaire and his wife gave to a New York magazine. I closed the interview window and pulled up Google to check out the billionaire couple she referenced. Brice and Imani Richardson. As I browsed the article, I found myself rolling my eyes. *Let Bree tell it, friends to lovers is a scam.* It does work with the right person. And the Richardsons proved it. I chuckled.

Pulling out my notebook, I decided to do my morning pages. I wasn't regular with it, but I liked doing a brain dump before I prayed and started my day. When I opened the teal-colored notebook, the quote my parents used to drum in my ear stared me dead in the face. Over the years, I desensitized myself to it. Today, looking at it, shame washed over me. They had such high hopes for me.

I had let one mishap shatter my perception of them and send me into a rebellious spiral. With all the regret I toted around, I still couldn't do the one thing they'd asked. I wasn't living intensely, neither was I loving loudly, and laughter was a hit and miss. I'd failed at a lot, but time was rolling by, and I had yet to make them proud. I could do better and that's exactly what I was going to do.

~

"Jasmine Marie Bowman, the last time I saw you was in July. I know that job is not keeping you that busy."

I was in my car in Asili Plaza listening to my aunt berate me for my second cancelled visit since last Fourth of July. The Bowmans always did something for the community during MLK day and I'd missed it. It was somewhat work related, but if I was being all the way honest, I just didn't want to go. Los Angeles had too many painful memories, so I avoided home when I could. I wasn't in the mood to pretend like I was okay, so I skipped the event.

My eyes darted from the time on my dashboard to the storefront I was scoping out. I was here earlier than my appointed time, just to see the traffic. I first learned of Floral Elegance a few months after I moved to Atlanta. I loved everything about it and for a split second I allowed myself to dream. Dream of one like it. One to call my own. This shopping complex was one of the premier complexes in Atlanta and from what I read, Black owned. Most of the businesses were too. Life took back over, and the dream faded.

Two days ago, with a renewed desire to live intensely and bold, I went online and saw that the store was for sale. My heart leapt in my chest. After calling to ensure it was real, I immediately asked for an appointment. Now, instead of working through lunch as I did most times at work, I flew out of there once the clock struck twelve. What I thought would be a quick check in with my aunt had now turned into a ten-minute session of guilt trip with a side of disappointment.

"Aunty, I really have been busy. I promise I'll make time to fly out. But I—"

"Have to go…"

I giggled because she thought she knew me. I really wasn't running game this time. I had to go. She told me she missed me, and I should really make time to come home. I told her that I loved her before asking her to kiss Ella for me.

After she sucked her teeth and rolled her eyes, she said. "That, young lady, you'll have to do yourself. Until her mother comes home, she gets no love."

"Aunty, come on, don't do Ella like that—" The rest of my whining was cut short when I saw the door to the flower shop open and the person I knew as the owner shook someone's hand. It was giving "nice doing business with you" vibes and I wasn't here for it.

"Aunty, I have to go. I love you." I disconnected the call, picked up my bag and folder, and got out of the car.

I scurried across the wet parking lot and pulled the door open. The chime alerted the lady who sat up front. The mix of fragrances hit me all at once. Instead of overwhelm, a peace rose up within me and I felt right at home. I told the lady why I was here, and she asked me to take a seat while she called to the back.

Instead of doing that, I decided to walk around a little. The shop had changed a bit from when I was in here a year ago. Different sizes and shapes of vases lined the window area. The design table and cooler were further to the left corner of the store. As I looked around, I thought of so many things I could do and what I wanted to preserve. I had recently taken some classes on making luxury balloon designs and the space in the corner could serve as a display.

"Tell me why you want it."

I blinked a few times. Ms. Ruby's question caught me off guard. I'd been escorted back a few minutes ago. Now I sat in front of a petite woman who was the cause of the sweat in my palms. She looked to be in her late sixties, same as my aunt. Her silver-colored mane was in a low ponytail and she had glasses perched on her nose. She had on a simple floral blouse over a red skirt that swept the floor.

I rubbed my palms against my jeans, lowering my eyes to my lap. I had a whole folder full of my designs, experience, and plans. I also wrote a few points on how I would maintain some of her legacy while forging one of my own. What I wasn't prepared for was to explain my motive.

"I want to make my parents proud," was the first thing that came to my head. Judging from the pointed look she gave me, it wasn't a good one.

"Then I can't sell it to you." She stood.

My stomach fell and my heart thumped in my chest. I was about to respond, but didn't have to because she still had the floor.

"Nothing you do because of the need to please others will ever succeed." She paused. "You know why?"

Again, my answer didn't come fast enough, so she helped me out.

"The desire must burn deep from within. A desire to use your gifts to serve others. Floral Elegance was built with a desire to spread joy. To brighten up the faces of others while being a ray of sunshine in the community it inhabits. I would rather close its doors than sell it to someone who wants to use it to prove a point."

I found my voice and stood. "What…Wait, no."

Ms. Ruby sat, and I followed suit. I bent my head, gathering strength to expose myself to a stranger. Lifting my head, I pushed back a loose curl that fell in my face and spoke. "Truthfully, I don't even know if owning a flower shop would make them proud. They knew my love for nature and flowers, but I always talked about being a corporate executive." A wry smile plastered my face as I caught a tear forming in the corner of my eye.

I hated this.

"All I really know is that they wanted me to live to my fullest potential. Live with intensity, loving as loud as I can while not forgetting to laugh. They recited that mantra to me almost daily. Back then, I thought it was them getting on my case. Now, I know they wanted it for me because they had it for themselves. I've failed miserably at it. A friend convinced me it's not too late for a reset. I'm asking for my reset."

Silence ensued and I was prepared for Ms. Ruby to sympathize with me and send me on my way. Instead, she said, "When did they pass?"

"Eleven years ago," I whispered. I really wanted to get off this topic.

"I understand the weight of feeling like a disappointment. It's one of the reasons I'm closing and moving up north to be closer to my daughter. She moved there years ago and because of family strife, we've been estranged."

Revealing so much caused sadness to consume me. I wasn't sure how to respond. I had no words to offer.

She sighed. "I had someone offer 170,000 for it. Your intent letter had 110,000. In as much—"

"I'll pay 180," I blurted out. "I can put ten thousand down now."

I'd done my research. This complex was a high traffic one with elite clientele. This shop was a community staple. Some of my clients over the years always told me they'd follow me anywhere. I'd still have to put in the work to attract new customers. But, I'd be crazy to not grab this store with both hands.

My only problem was I had put my foot in my mouth. Because I didn't have $180,000 to give anyone. After my parents passed, I had spent a whole year coasting with no real income coming in. What they left me had also dwindled considerably over the years. I had a savings, but nowhere close to $180,000.

Ms. Ruby stood. "I like you, young lady. I'll take the for sale sign down. If I don't see you back here by the end of June, it will be back up for sale."

I squealed. My cheeks hurt from how wide the grin on my face was. I thanked Ms. Ruby and left. I stood in front of the store, taking in the environment. I saw a lady walking a few feet away.

"Excuse me," I called out and she turned. With hurried steps, I went to meet her. "Hi, sorry to bother you, but do you have a store here?"

The lady gave me a once over then a small smile appeared across her face. "And you are?"

I stretched out my hand to her. "I'm so sorry. I'm Jasmine. I'm looking to own a storefront here."

She shook my hand. "Hi, I'm Reign. I own the skincare store a few doors down."

"How is the location?"

She sized me up again then shrugged. "Very high traffic area, no crime. At least not in the time I've been here. And it's owned by us." She pointed to the back of her hand, indicating Black.

I thanked her and walked to my car. I pulled out my phone and shot Aubree a text.

Can't believe I'm doing this but send me the info for the renting thing.

I got in my car and bowed my head on the steering wheel. "Father, I have no clue, but You do, and I trust you."

5

ARINZE

arch rolled into April before I received an email from Rent A Bae, informing me a match had been found. So here I was, on a mid-Saturday morning, walking into Stuffed Comfort. Instead of a formal restaurant for a first date; the agency decided on a casual event for me to meet my "prospect."

Stuffed Comfort was a local charity that assembled stuffed toys for babies who'd been abandoned. From what I gathered, the toys were distributed among foster homes, orphanages, and local hospitals. The higher end stuffed toys like the ones we were supposed to be making today were put up for auction and the funds put back into the community. The charity relied heavily on volunteers to achieve their monthly targets.

For an assembly warehouse, I was struck by the air of casual sophistication of the large rectangular room. A blend of bright and earth toned paint covered the walls with various pieces of abstract artwork hanging from them. The inbuilt shelves along the walls housed various stuffed animals. The furnishing was a mix of contemporary and abstract pieces. In the center of the room were ten assembly tables, each containing what I assumed were the tools and materials to assemble stuffed animals of various shapes and sizes.

Pulling down my hat, I located the check-in window and walked over.

"Hi, welcome to Stuffed Comfort," the attendant greeted.

Sporting a small smile, I presented the reservation paper the agency sent me. "Hello, I have a reservation number."

The young lady took the paper from me and began clicking away on the computer in front of her. As I waited, my thoughts traveled back to the lengthy process that led up to this moment. I understood, and even appreciated the discretion, detailed steps, and overall due diligence taken in screening the "renter" and the "prospect."

Rent A Bae demonstrated that the comfort and safety of all parties was their priority. However, the process had been so time consuming that I was almost tempted to give up. I doubted I'd completed so many forms even when I was buying my house. I respected their thoroughness.

According to their terms and conditions, I had to sign waivers, giving them permission to check the validity of my family. After everything checked out, I moved to stage two. Here I had to provide my likes, dislikes, needs, wants, and duration of the contract. They also sent over a copy of the non-disclosure agreement the other party would be signing. For security reasons, names weren't given beforehand. This made it safe for either party to pull out if they wanted to without the fear of being followed, stalked, or harassed. Their name I still found laughable, but they had a well-oiled operation.

The attendant handed me a wristband and buzzed me into the main area. The loud hum of the air conditioner almost drowned out the soft melody of R&B classics playing from the sound system. Giving a nod of acknowledgement to other volunteers, I located our designated table.

I bobbed my head to the tune of "This Is How We Do It" by Montell Jordan, and my eyes roamed the room, anticipating the arrival of my date. We were supposed to begin in a few minutes, and she had yet to arrive. According to the instructions, she'd have on the same black pin I currently had on the lapel of my blazer.

In the past weeks, I'd been so caught up with work that I hadn't let myself dwell on this moment. Now trepidation bounced around in the pit of my stomach. For this to work, the person had to be all in. My grandmother could smell a phony from a mile away. My trip was in four weeks, so I had no time to do this again. It was either this or hurt the old lady because she definitely wouldn't like my response to her pick for me.

When I got the match profile, the woman who was referred to as "Optimal Match" was more than optimal. In fact, on paper she looked perfect. For some reason, that bothered me. Was it an autobot at work or did someone like that really exist?

"Ladies and gentlemen, please take your place behind your designated tables. We'll get started in five minutes," the coordinator announced.

Retrieving my phone from my back pocket, I scanned through my emails. Maybe I'd missed a notification of cancellation. She should've been here by now. There was none. In case of a no-show, my mind ran through all the work I'd set aside that I could now get done. It also went to a contingency plan I really didn't want to consider.

Vivienne.

She wasn't what I would consider a friend, but she also wasn't as distant as an acquaintance. The only time we really contacted each other was when the other was in a date bind for an event. Over the years, we'd slipped into a weird, comfortable space with no expectations. I wanted to keep it that way, hence contacting her would be my absolute…

The vaguely familiar, sensual scent of a mango citrus

fragrance ticked my senses. My chest tightened and my stomach flipped in jubilee.

Her.

Lifting my eyes, I came face to face with the woman I'd become upset with for invading my thoughts. No matter how much I tried to push away the memory of our night together, she kept inserting herself in my head. From her turned up, full lips, wrinkled nose, crease on her forehead, and frost in her eyes, I could tell she wasn't too happy to see me either.

I took advantage of her shocked state to allow my eyes to roam her lithe frame. Her hair was still the way I remembered it, spiral black curls with light brown highlights. Half of it was in a bun while the rest fell on her shoulders. Her blue and white off the shoulder short sleeved blouse was knotted in the font. The delicate fabric rested on hip hugging blue jean Capri pants. On her feet were some white logo slip-on sneakers, with a delicate anklet on her left leg.

"Ugh...you."

The disgust dripping from her tone pulled me out of the trance I was in. Without taking my eyes off her, I said. "Nice to see you again, Jasmine."

I didn't know if she'd gotten rid of the man she'd been arguing with three months ago. Considering what she was here for, I asked myself if it even still mattered.

6

JASMINE

My eyes widened as I tried to decipher whether this was God's work or the enemy trying to steal my peace. What in the world? Out of all the men in Atlanta, well the available ones, it had to be him? The scream that couldn't pass my lips broke loose in my head. He was still so fine. Avoiding his piercing brown eyes, I gave him a once over. Everything about him was just as I remembered. A memory that stayed in my head, no matter how far away I wanted it to go.

He had on a black bucket hat, so I wasn't sure if he still had a bald head. The connecting moustache and beard that framed his full lips were freshly trimmed. His simple fit of black jeans, a burnt orange button down shirt with matching orange loafers finished off his look.

Handcrafted by God.

Stepping into Stuffed Comfort, that unforgettable prickling sensation caused the hairs on my skin to rise. There was no way *he* was here. I always turned my nose up at those romance books talking about instant connection. But this right here—the pull Arinze had on me—was making a fool out of me. In Montego Bay, I'd chalked the feeling up to the romantic atmosphere of the wedding and ushering in the new year. But here it was again, in a freaking toy warehouse of all places. The dichotomy of the calming and electrifying effect his presence solicited caused my body to react, and I absolutely hated it.

I'd had a speech prepared for him for about four months now, and I was prepared to give it. My spiel was halted by the voice behind me.

"Okay, once again, welcome everyone," the instructor spoke.

The corner of Arinze's mouth shifted into a grin. Rolling my eyes, I stuffed my purse in the cubby under the table. If only I had spoken sooner, I would've stormed out and would be on my way back home by now. Or if I had gotten here early as planned, I would've spotted him and turned around. Now I was stuck, and I blamed Aubree and my GPS. One with an obsession with my attire and the other for failing to reroute twice when I got lost.

"Glad you all could join us today. My name is Matt and I'll be your instructor for the session." He followed his introduction by listing a few housekeeping items. Next, he went over the materials and expectations for the day.

There were ten tables and each of us were to meet a goal of ten finished box sets in the two-hour time frame. I glanced at the table covered with scissors, glue guns, buttons, knit pre-sewn material, cotton, and other scrap pieces of cloth. The boxes, which were at another table, already had shoes, blankets, rattles, and story books in them. All that was missing were the stuffed toys we were making.

This was for babies. What kind of person would I be to walk out? My best strategy would be to ignore him as much as possible. Once the instructor left, completely ignoring Arinze, I picked up a pre-sewn, knit encasement. I reached for the scissors, but they fell on the table, and the clatter drew attention. I let out a breath, unable to contain my frustration.

Arinze's gaze burned the side of my face. Walking closer to

me, he whispered. "Is there something you'd like to get off your chest?"

His dangerous, raspy baritone washed over me, temporarily leaving me speechless. I glanced over at him. When a smirk crossed his face, my good sense quickly returned. Mr. "That wasn't a request" called himself meticulously taking me on a high into the wee hours of New Year's morning. When we walked to my room, I could feel his energy shift. He gave me some story about needing to get to bed and he'd see me in the morning.

Did he? No. He ghosted me. I was fine on my own, but he had to lay his lips on me, almost taking my soul with him, then left me high and dry.

"No," came my terse response.

He licked his bottom lip and simpered. "Sounds like you do. Holding grudges isn't healthy. You need to let it go."

"Can you leave me alone?"

This was a team effort, so I knew I sounded ridiculous, but if he could be quiet, maybe I could trick my mind and body into believing he wasn't there. Their betrayal stung.

He rolled up some cotton and scrap material and handed them to me. "Your vibe says you do."

I glanced at his hand. Ignoring it, I leaned over to collect my own scraps. "You should be the expert on misreading vibes."

Arinze placed his hand over mine, pausing my movement. Heat traveled up my arm and I snatched away. That didn't deter him because this man walked behind me and leaned over my shoulder. I felt every part of him. "You see all these people?" He pointed to the other couples. "They're working together, meanwhile you're here pouting and sulking. You're refusing my help, and we haven't made one single toy. He moved to my side. "I take it you're upset with me…now tell me why."

I needed to get it together. I opened my mouth to deny. "Look…"

"Okay, that's it. Come with me." He grabbed my hand, almost dragging me along as we left the common area.

I thought we were going to the lobby area. But no, this man escorted me outside and backed me against the side of the building. His arms came up to my sides, trapping me in place. Apart from music, horns and cars zipping by in the background, we stood in silence. His eyes left mine and roamed my body. I knew I had on clothes, but under his gaze, I felt naked. We were so close that the coolness of his breath mingled with mine. When his teeth grazed his lower lip, I cleared my throat.

"Can you move?" I almost couldn't hear myself.

"I can," he said, but made no attempt to move.

I raised my brow. "Now?" My voice was much stronger.

"Depends."

I shook my head. "On what? Arinze, move…"

"Only if you'd be honest and tell me why you're upset with me."

No way was I going to tell him I was mad because he left me horny and disappeared. His rejection stung, but that was my problem. I shrugged. "I don't like you. What? You never ran across someone who wasn't affected by your charm?"

He chuckled and stepped back. "I have no problem with people not liking me. But I know for a fact you do." He caressed my cheek with the back of his hand. "By the way your breath hitches, these goosebumps on your smooth skin and your shaky voice, I'd say you like me more than a little bit."

His arrogance annoyed and awakened things in me that I'd long since forgotten. Before I could formulate a response, he continued.

"Don't be alarmed. I like you too. So, tell me the problem so I can either explain, clarify, apologize or all three. Then we can get back to making toys for the kids."

A sadness washed over me. I could kiss Luxe Petals goodbye. Pretending to be anything to him wasn't going to work in my favor. My attraction to him was intense and could potentially turn into something more. That, I couldn't afford. "For real, I'm tripping. I didn't expect to see you. That's all."

He raised his brow, clearly indicating he didn't believe a word I said. Well, that was all he was going to get. I'd done too much already. "Besides I don't know you well enough to like you."

"If that's your story, I'mma let you tell it." His hands slid into his pockets. "But we need to fix this not knowing me thing. My woman has to know all parts of me."

"Pretend. And in case you've forgotten, there's a three-date trial period before anything is finalized."

Laughing, he took my hand and led me back inside. "Okay, come on. Let's get to know each other." He glanced over at me. "I might end up not really liking you."

As we entered, after a quick perusal of the other tables, I figured we were about four toys behind. I grunted. I hated to lose.

Arinze must have read my thoughts. He turned to me once we were behind our table. "This is your fault," he said.

"Yeah, whatever. Hurry up, we gotta catch up."

Now that the tension between us was at a manageable level, we were able to work in sync. For the next several minutes, I mapped out a plan and Arinze and I got to work. In comfortable silence, we worked as a team. I put the stuffed animal together while Arinze glued on the eyes, buttons, and ribbon around its neck.

With a couple of toys down, Arinze spoke. "Ask away."

"Full name," I asked. I regretted not getting that information that night. It would've made it easier to Google him. Then again, most of the stuff online was false. I knew that firsthand.

"Arinze Kayode Kalu."

"Jasmine Marie Bowman. How old are you?"

"Thirty-seven, you?"

"Thirty-one. Career?" I knew he was a celebrity, but I had no idea what he did.

"Actor and movie consultant. You?"

"Wait, you mean movie, movie?"

He chuckled. "Is there any other kind?"

I looked around and saw that everyone was either minding their business or oblivious to who he was.

"I guess not, but where's your entourage? Don't y'all go around with people all the time?"

"I don't. I have one muscle and he's off for the night."

"If these women here find out who you are and try to mob you, I can't help you, buddy."

"You'll leave me to my fate? Won't even stay to help me escape?"

"Nope."

He put his hand on his chest. "I'm hurt and here I was thinking that as my woman, you got my back."

I laughed.

"Anyway, unless they're into war action films, they probably won't know who I am."

He was pretty laid back and didn't radiate "celebrity." He must be one of those D list actors. I made a mental note to Google him later. From the watch on his wrist, it didn't look like he was hurting for money, but then again, people rented all kinds of stuff to put on a show.

The rest of our time flew by so fast. We had so much fun laughing and getting to know each other. Arinze didn't seem to take himself seriously, neither was he insecure in his masculinity. That was obvious when he allowed me to lead in the building of our toys. He had no problem assisting and following my lead. I found myself comparing him to Derrick who thought we were in competition with one another.

During our conversation, I found out that Arinze had a solid relationship with God and his family was a close second. His number one love language was physical touch. When I told him mine was acts of service, he didn't seem surprised.

His favorite time of day was late at night. He loved Afrobeats and country music, and his favorite color was orange. We loved the same movies, and both of us would prefer a chilled environment rather than the bumping and grinding of a club. The more we talked, the more I discovered he checked all the boxes I used to have. Aubree was right. I didn't allow myself to love because it was too painful to lose. I made up my mind to enjoy this time with him because after this, I was going to make sure I didn't see him again.

At the end of the day, Arinze and I came in last place. We had produced the least number of toys. When the results were called, he nudged me playfully blaming me for "Naija carrying last." Apparently, that was based on a catch phrase Nigerians used about them never coming in behind anyone. We did win the trophy for best quality. Even though we had fun, we both were determined to make sure each toy was worthy of display. After cleaning up our stations, we left.

Once we got to my car, I leaned against it, now ready to ask the question I'd held in all day. "Arinze–"

"Nze."

"Huh?"

"Call me Nze. That's what my family and friends call me. I'm Arinze to the world, or to my mom and grandmother when they're upset with me."

I smiled. "In that case, call me Jazzy."

"Does everyone call you that?"

I nodded. "Those close to me."

"Then I'll stick to Jas. I have some other names for you if you like." The look in his eye resembled the one he had months ago when he stalked over to me like I was his prey. I cleared my throat and he grinned. His cocky was sexy. He knew exactly what he was doing too.

Pushing the ungodly images in my head to the side, I rolled my eyes and straightened my back. "Tell me why someone like you needs to rent a bae?"

His brow rose. "Someone like me?"

I shrugged. "Yeah, seemingly nice and kind, God fearing, thriving career," I pointed to his watch. "You don't seem to be in need financially and you're easy on the eyes and sexy." That last part came out before I could stop myself. If I were two shades lighter, my skin would show a tinge of red from embarrassment.

"You think I'm sexy and handsome, Jas?"

"Can you forget that and answer the question?"

He placed his hand on his chest. "I, for one, think it's a momentous occasion. Can I celebrate it, please? You went from not liking me, to 'you're sexy and handsome'."

The gleam in his eyes annoyed me. "You're not going to make this easy."

"Nope. But for the record, I think you're gorgeous." He placed his hands on my waist. "Sexy goes without saying."

I lowered my eyes briefly before lifting them again. "Thank you."

"To answer your question, I'm not seeing anyone, and my time is otherwise occupied. I don't have the capacity to spend time with someone, get to know her well enough to want to introduce her to my family."

"So, what's the rush? Get one when you have the time."

"I would, but—"

My phone rang cutting him off. I would've sent it to voice-mail, but it was the ringtone I set for Aunty Delia. Doing a mental calculation of the time in L.A, I looked up at Arinze.

"Excuse me, I have to take this."

He nodded, stepping away to give me privacy.

"Ella is sick," my aunt said when the call connected.

Worry snaked through me. "How sick?"

"The doctor strongly recommends you come see her."

I disconnected the call and with shaky hands fumbled through my purse for my keys. My vision was blurry from tears dancing in my eyes. Suddenly I felt his presence, then his hands halted my erratic movements. I didn't have time to explain away the confusion etched on his face. I needed to go. Ella was all I had left of them. I wasn't ready to lose her too.

"I have to go. I'm sorry, but I have to get out of here." A tear rolled down my cheek.

Arinze enveloped me in a brief hug. "Jas, you're shaking. I need you to calm down for me. Tell me what you need."

I released a labored breath. "I have to go."

He cupped my face in his hands. "I got that. Go where?"

"L.A."

He took my keys. "Do you trust me?"

I didn't know if I did or not. But I knew he provided me a sense of calm, so I nodded.

"Then let's go."

"My car…"

"I'll get someone to handle it. Let's go, so I can get you to L.A." With his arm draped over my shoulder, he guided me to his car. Once I was properly secured in, Arinze got in the car and drove.

I stared at him. In response, he squeezed my hand. He merged into traffic, taking us to the airport. He didn't ask who, what or how. He jumped into action immediately, to make sure I was taken care of. I had no idea what to do with that. And an even lesser idea of what to do with him.

7

ARINZE

omething wasn't adding up.

That thought had been circulating in my head since yesterday evening. From the balcony of my L.A penthouse, the fresh breezy smell from the beach below wafted up my nostrils. I took in a deep breath and exhaled. The morning air attempted to clear the fog I was in. Numerous birds littered the air, chirping away to their destinations.

Wearing only pajama bottoms, I leaned against the cool steel of the railing. The events of the previous day were on a loop in my mind. I was still processing the fact that Jasmine was my optimal match. I mean, where does that happen?

Baby girl was seriously upset with me. I might've known why, but since she didn't say nothing, I let it rock. I can't lie, we had a really nice time. It's one thing to share a kiss, no matter how dynamic it might be. It was a whole other thing to vibe with her on a non-sexual level. Talking about everything and nothing while making toys with her was the most chill time I'd ever had with a woman.

My dad taught me to look out for how people treat the people they don't really need. Jasmine was polite and kind to a degree

I've hardly seen. When we went to the food stand during the break, and they messed up her order the first time, I almost wanted to duck. Flashbacks of Chantel came flooding through. Seconds went by and I didn't hear insults or see packets of condiments flying through the air. Jasmine accepted the apology of the attendant and waited for him to fix her another nacho bowl.

I was attracted to her no doubt, but this woman had me seriously out of character. I needed to take a step back and look at this for what it was. She signed up with an agency that matched people for personal or business reasons. I was not sure if this was a regular thing for her.

I took a sip from the glass of water in my hand. My eyes focused on the rising sun. I knew it was hypocritical to think that way. I signed up for the same thing. But it was what it was. Was this a regular for her? Anyway, all my reservations flew out the window when I saw her tears.

I was the guy who calculated my every move. Took in all available information, then weighed the pros and cons before I acted. All that was gone when she began falling apart in my arms. The only thing I could focus on was doing whatever I could to ease her pain and provide her comfort. I drove like a madman trying to get her to the airport. She kept mumbling to herself that she couldn't take another loss.

L.A wasn't on my itinerary until the end of the week, but I couldn't let her get on the flight alone. As luck would have it, there was a Delta flight available, so I got us two, first-class tickets. Chuckling to myself, I remembered how alert she suddenly became when I presented my card for payment. Then it was all kinds of "I got it," "You don't have to do that," and "You've done enough." Of course, her objections fell on deaf ears.

As we waited for takeoff, I heard her on the phone with her friend who I now knew as Aubree. I didn't mean to eavesdrop, but she was right on me. I had pulled her close to me. Her head was on my chest and my arm was around her. She didn't object to the comfort I provided. For me, it felt familiar.

Ella must mean a lot to her. She was crying and carrying on about how she couldn't lose her. Did she have a daughter? A little sister? Or was Ella her mom? Jasmine was so distraught that I couldn't ask the questions I wanted answers to. I'm guessing the food we had, the activity we'd done, and all that crying tired her out. Soon as she hung up, she whispered a "Thank you," snuggled into me and was out.

When we landed, my usual car service was waiting. She gave me the address to one of the poshest residential areas in LA. When we arrived, after driving through the winding driveway, we got to a house that was seated on at least two acres of land. She refused me walking her to the door. I protested but gave in when she offered her number, so I'd know she was okay.

I watched as an older woman opened the massive door and welcomed her in. Then I left. I was aware that most people who signed up to provide dating services did it because of the financial gain. Jasmine didn't seem to need any money, so I was floored. After touching base with my cousins, I took a warm shower, did a little writing, and then hit the sheets, calling it a night.

Again, something wasn't adding up.

Walking back into my living room, I picked up the remote and turned the television to ESPN. In the early years of my career, Los Angeles was home. When I finally made my first million, I invested in a very lucrative stock portfolio and bought my home in Atlanta. The spacious, open plan here, was one of the selling points for me when my realtor sent this condo to me. It came with recessed lighting, soaring ceilings, and a fireplace. I was on the top floor of a high-rise that overlooked the ocean.

Although I could afford to hire someone to decorate my space, my mother and sisters decided that they would experiment on my space. Any time I actually got to enjoy my three-bedroom, two-bath home, I had to give them their props. The African centric décor came together perfectly with the cream-colored sofas and chocolate accent wall in the parlor. Entering the kitchen, I opened the stainless steel refrigerator, deciding on whether to cook or order something.

I pulled out the buzzing phone from my pocket. I tugged on my beard, grinning at Ciara's dry response.

OK. Boss.

She never called me boss unless she was mad at me. It was Sunday, her rest and meditation day. I tried to make it mine too, but what I needed couldn't wait. I'd texted her earlier to move up any appointments she could. There was no sense in waiting until Friday when I really was supposed to be here. Responding with my thanks, I used the opportunity to check on Jasmine.

Good morning, Jas. How are you feeling? Call me.

My housekeeper was expecting me, so the fridge was stocked. I decided to make an omelet and plantains to calm down the hunger building inside me. I put all the ingredients on the granite countertop and propped my phone up against a canister so I could FaceTime Cheta. He answered on the second ring.

"Nze, do I need to call Aunty B? *O gini di?*" Cheta asked when he came into view. He moved away from his friends I could see in the background.

Laughing, I positioned the kettle under the running water. "*Nna mehn...* first, where's Jidenna? Today is Sunday. No brunch?"

"Nah, Ju has a cold, and you know how he is when she's ill. I'll check on them later." He was now on the deck in his backyard. "This was supposed to be an *arrangee*. How are you flying out to L.A with her?" His face contorted. "You know I was busy yesterday. So, I heard you, but you gotta give it to me again."

The way Cheta said busy, I knew it had something to do with a woman. He was currently in some hot water with his management team because of a woman, but still, he couldn't stay away from them. I've called him to order before, but he's grown so I let him handle his own business. So instead of giving him a hard time, I told him about Jasmine. Since nothing came of me and Jasmine in Jamaica, I saw no reason to tell my cousins about her then. Telling Cheta about it now had him in a range of emotions. Disbelief, suspicion, and skepticism.

"Are you sure she didn't Google you?" he asked. "Don't you find this suspicious? *Check am na.* She knew you were a celeb from the wedding. I'm sure about that. Even if you didn't give her any kind of information, how hard would it have been to type Arinze in Google and your picture appears?"

I broke the eggs, cut up the vegetables and sliced the plantain as Cheta continued to lay out all his conspiracy theories. One thing we did for each other was go hard. I didn't expect anything less from him, but I wasn't stupid. I knew anything could happen, but I didn't get that vibe from her. The shock and anger she showed when we came face to face let me know immediately, she had no idea who she was meeting with.

I told Cheta this to which this joker responded, "Nze, *hapụ ihe ahụ.* People can lie. I'm sure that was a performance. Don't trust these women."

I laughed at him. "There you go trying to project your issues on me."

"Have you forgotten Chantel?" he asked.

"I do remember Chantel. That's why I'm cautious, but that doesn't mean I have trust issues."

Cheta grunted.

I flipped the frying plantain over and added, "You know she's been hitting my DM a lot."

"Wait. What?" he growled.

His reaction was expected. Jidenna's would probably be worse. I met Chantel during the rise of my career. I'd gotten a break, starring in a movie with one of Hollywood's big wigs. One night at an industry party, this beautiful woman spilled her drink on my shirt. We spent the rest of the night getting to know one another. She came with someone but left with me. That should have been my red flag. It was a red flag, but I ignored it. She was show stopping gorgeous with a figure to match, and I loved having her on my arm.

After a few casual dates, we became exclusive. Then the demands started. She owned an online boutique and wanted me to introduce her to people in my circle. I wanted my girl to come up, so I did. But that wasn't enough. She wanted folks with deeper pockets, and I had no access to the names she was mentioning. This led to the fights and arguments. Then things quieted down.

I felt things were looking up for us. I'd planned to ask her to fly to Nigeria with me to meet the whole family. Cheta and Jidenna couldn't stand her, but they were respectful. When my sister came to visit me, she wasn't too happy about Chantel either. But I forged ahead. I was going to ask her to marry me. Until one day at a gala for a charity that we attended together, the bottom fell out.

In, walked this belligerent man, claiming I stole his wife. He made a big spectacle apologizing and professing his love for Chantel. I stood with eyes wide open as I watched the scandal unfold. I couldn't have written a better horror film. I was in a whole love triangle that I knew nothing about. He punched me and my reflexes took over. He must not have known I was Naija and an Airman. I beat the pulp out of him. None of this Hollywood stuff mattered the moment another man put his hands on me. Security did their best to stop me, but I blacked out.

As expected, I was taken into custody. My face was plastered everywhere. The news got back home. My parents were in panic mode and the blogs had a field day. With me being ex-military, everyone spun their own narrative. Some said I should've exercised self-control while others said I was unbalanced, suffering from the effects of my time in the US Armed Forces.

Chantel went on about her business. She didn't even try to clear my name. I lived in the nightmare for almost a year. And now, after five whole years, she pops back up six months ago.

"Nze?"

Cheta shouted my name, right on time considering my plantains had started to go from golden brown to black.

"Wassup?"

"I'm the last person to speak on love—"

"Wait a minute. I never mentioned being in love. Am I attracted to her? Bad, but love...no."

"Okay then, the wedding is next month. If you and her have a vibe, and she agrees, flow with the arrangement to get Mama off your back." He shook his head. "You don't even know if she got a baby. Ain't nothing wrong with a baby, but if she tucked her away in L.A and is living in Atlanta, that's a character flaw."

I flung my head back and laughed. "Man. Get off my phone sounding like Dr. Phil."

"I'm just saying. You might want to find out about the child's father. You don't want another crazy idiot popping up." He laughed at his own silliness. "This time for sure Aunty B and Adaugo will carry her name to the native doctor for some spells."

I gasped. "I'm telling. You saying my mother goes to a *babalawo*."

"Aunty B and I are cool, so I'll deny you. I'm only putting possibilities out there."

"Hmmm..." I continued to fix my breakfast while he updated me about his week, and I did the same with mine. We were all we had in America, so we made an oath that no matter how busy we got, we'd stay updated on each other. We were our brother's keeper.

Jas: Good morning. I'm good.

Jasmine's text notification popped up. I disconnected from Cheta and opened it. Three dots appeared indicating she was typing another message. I placed my phone on the counter, plated my food, and prepared some tea. Sitting at the island, I said grace while her next message came through.

Jas: Words aren't enough to thank you. Do you have any plans today??

The corner of my lips turned up in a smile. The images in my head were unlawful, and I knew what I was thinking wasn't what she meant, but I decided to mess with her.

I'm flattered but my naked body is reserved for my future wife.

She replied with a couple of laughing emojis. **You wish.**

I sent her some laughing emojis back.

I'm glad you're laughing. You scared me yesterday. Everything good?

I'm better. So, are you free?

Whatchu got in mind?

This is my city, so I want to take you somewhere special.

I laughed.

Girl this is my stomping ground. Whatchu wanna show me?

I know you're an actor and all, but I grew up here. This is my last time asking, are you free?

I'm all yours, baby.

Hmmm. Okay, I can come to you, or you can come to me.

I'll be there. An hour good?

Perfect.

I was glad she reached out and I yearned to be in her presence again. Something that had been bugging me and Cheta brought up as well still plagued my mind.

Aye. Lemme ask you something.

Wassup?

Who is Ella?

She started to type. The dots kept dancing, but her response wasn't coming through. Either she was sending a long response, or she kept deleting what she was writing. My heart raced at the possibility that it could be the latter. That would most definitely mean she was trying to craft the right lie or decide how much she wanted me to know.

My horse.

I blinked a couple of times and read it again. I know she didn't just say that she had me so worried about her over an animal. Nah, all that crying she was doing wasn't over an animal. I couldn't text my response. I was hot, so I dialed.

Three rings later and her face appeared on my screen. At first, my words got lost in her bright eyes. The droplet of water running down the side of her face let me know that she'd probably just taken a shower. She panned out the camera, and I could see she had on a blue terry robe and was rubbing lotion on her legs.

"Hellooooo," she said with a faint smile.

"Hey, beautiful. Okay, I need to hear you say it. Your horse is what had you about to lose your mind?" I lifted my brow. I believed animal lovers did too much, but the show she put on last night had to have something deeper to it.

She stopped what she was doing and looked at me, her expression downcast. "You won't understand…"

Nodding, I said, "Yeah, you right. But I'm willing to be enlightened."

She tittered. "It's silly."

"Let me be the judge of that."

Her hand went to the back of her neck, and she sighed. "Ella is my parents' last gift to me. She was a surprise."

My chest tightened at the shakiness of her voice. The brightness in her eyes was replaced with a pained gaze. It mirrored the look in Jidenna's eyes on occasion. "Where are they?"

She let out a labored breath. "Dead." A lone tear rolled down her check.

"Get dressed. See you in an hour."

Jasmine didn't give a verbal response, rather she shifted her eyes to me and simply nodded. Behind her sad eyes, I could detect a hint of gratitude and… relief.

I disconnected the call and went to tidy up the kitchen. Jasmine awakened the protector in me. I wanted to shield her from pain and shoulder her burdens. That part of me came with additional qualities I didn't think she, nor I was ready for. At least not now.

8

JASMINE

I'd accumulated so much junk.

I threw another blouse on the bed and my eyes darted to my phone. Shoot! He'd be here in twenty-five minutes and I didn't have a clue what to wear. I walked up to the mirror in the bedroom I'd occupied in my aunt's house after my parents died. I held up the blouse to my chest and twisted my lips. The Boyz to Men poster stared back at me through the mirror. My crushes way back then. That Michael knew he was fine.

My alarm went off. It was alerting me to the twenty-minute countdown I gave myself. I didn't know why I was trying so hard to impress him. Neither did I want to think about it. If I did, I'd be so deep in my head that I wouldn't be able to find my way out. Rummaging through my closet, I thought about the events of the past couple of hours.

"Do you trust me?"

That was his question. Although I wasn't sure, in that moment I said yes. Arinze stormed into action so fast that my head began to spin. I knew I was getting bad at comparing Arinze to Derrick, but I couldn't help it. It's like they were night and day. Before I moved to Chicago, he'd been hounding me about getting rid of Ella. But I couldn't do it.

Because of the time difference, when Arinze and I arrived, it was late afternoon. I was able to meet with the vet. My baby's distress caused my heart to tighten. The sheen on her deep brown coat was duller. Her sharp black eyes were beady. From what the vet said, the lingering complication from the virus she contracted some years ago was getting worse. She now had a tumor in her leg. The doctor gave her something to relieve the pain but advised he'd do an MRI to see how advanced it was, and if it had spread anywhere else.

In any case, her pain was excruciating. I had to think of the possibility of letting her go. I had cried so much until my aunty came and got me. This morning, after a quick breakfast, I walked the grounds to the shed where Ella stayed. I talked to my girl, reminiscing on the times we'd had together. The tears were gone, but thinking of why I was here, brought me back to Arinze.

The man was nice, so patient and understanding. I know I was being extra, but I was deathly afraid that something might happen to her before I got here. He didn't badger me at all. I found myself finding solace in his silent strength. I really thought he'd put me on the plane and be on his way, but when he got on the plane with me…stunned wasn't even the word.

I had to hurry up and get dressed. He was on his way and I was still standing here looking confused. I settled on a pair of dark blue, high waist jeans, a color block crop top, and a pair of Vans. I pulled my hair into a half updo. I pulled some tresses down so that they would frame my face, and then ran my fingers through my coils.

Arinze was already annoyed about me doing all that over a horse. I didn't want to hear his mouth about me always being late.

While we were making toys, he'd asked the reason I was fussing over flowers during the wedding in Jamaica. I thought he genuinely wanted to know. I was even flattered he remembered. Nope. According to him, he was noticing a pattern of my tardiness. A smile crossed my face when I remembered nudging his shoulder and rolling my eyes.

Another thing I got to do this morning was Google him. I was on the phone with Aubree while we did our investigation. The man I've been with didn't match his presence on the internet. He wasn't an A list actor, but this man was an actor, actor. His box office hits were impressive. The people I saw him mingling with on his Instagram page were Hollywood heavy hitters. From what I'd seen of him and his online profile, his humility was either an act, or he was really that modest. How he didn't walk around with "people" was amazing to me.

There were some articles about some scandal years ago, but I didn't pay those no mind. I knew exactly how the press could be. At the end of my investigation, I'd concluded I was going to kill Arinze. In all his talk about family, this man failed to tell me that the point guard for the Atlanta Harriers, Cheta Kalu, was his cousin.

"Whoever wrote *Standoff*, shouldn't have killed off Vison in the movie. He was a villain, but he needed redemption."

My ear tuned into people talking from downstairs. It was Uncle George. I grabbed my light jacket, cross body, and phone before darting out of my room. I knew Arinze just didn't walk up to the door without letting me know he was here. I almost ran into Aunty Delia.

"I didn't know you were going out."

I looked over the landing. Arinze looked up and winked at me. Those hazel eyes. He turned to my uncle and explained the reasoning behind killing whoever in a movie I was guessing he starred in.

"Errrm, yes Aunty. I—"

She grabbed my arm. "Is that the young man that brought you home yesterday?"

I nodded, trying to ear hustle at what Uncle George was telling Arinze. *No growing up stories please.*

"He's handsome. He sounds American, but I hear a faint accent," she said, cheesing at me.

My eyes darted downstairs again. "He's Nigerian-American, and don't get any ideas. He's just an acquaintance of mine."

"Your uncle was an acquaintance too, before—"

I kissed her cheek halting the story she was about to narrate. It was just in time too because I heard Uncle George asking Arinze what his intentions were. I think I gained wings and flew down the stairs. I kissed my uncle, told him I'd see him later and then dragged a laughing Arinze out of the house.

I swatted his shoulder as we strolled down the gravel pathway. "It's not funny. I'm so embarrassed."

"Don't be. Family…"

I turned around when his voice trailed off. I found him standing and nodding his head in obvious admiration and approval of what I had on.

"Really?"

"Really." He looked up to the sky. "Have you seen you? Good gracious God, I've seen beauty before, but this… Thank you."

The vibrations from my laughter had my stomach in knots. I was sure my aunt heard me. I used the opportunity to do an inventory of him as well. The dark gray jogger set had a patch of African print on the pocket and the side of the pants. I knew it was designer by the ZF logo on the pocket. He also wore a ball cap and some dark shades. For the first time, I noticed he looked like someone who was trying to hide his identity.

"Thank you. You don't look too bad yourself."

"Thank you."

As we approached his black truck, a dark skinned, bulky but well-toned man got out of the driver's seat. I think he was going to open the door, but before he could, Arinze spoke.

"I got it, Trent." Arinze opened the back door and I climbed in.

Seconds later, Arinze was in the backseat with me and made the introductions. Trent, who I now knew to be security, tipped his head toward me. I knew he said hello, but I promise, I didn't see his lips part. I was sorry for whoever crossed him. I wondered why the switch up, then I remembered, we were in L.A where I was sure Arinze was more well known, so it made sense.

Arinze took off his shades and the jacket of his jogger set. He twisted his body toward me. "So, Miss 'It's My Home,' where you taking me?"

"I know you're Hollywood and all. But you kinda grew up in Atlanta." We both chuckled. "Tell me you know how to skate?" I smiled at him.

He cocked his head and frowned. "You must be some kinda sucker for punishment."

"Why?"

He chuckled and the sound sent waves through my body. I was already trying to keep myself distracted from the pull of his now familiar scent and the way his short sleeves gripped his biceps. He leaned toward me.

"Jas, I will skate circles around you."

I raised my brows. "You think so?"

He brought his face closer to mine. "I know so. Ask about me in Cascade."

I nodded. Accepting the challenge, I turned to Trent and gave him the address to one of my favorite hangouts in Glendale.

Whatever Arinze thought he knew, I proved him wrong. Or he allowed me to. Whichever one, I won. He did initially skate circles around me. I chucked it up to his distracting presence. He did have a competitive streak, especially when we teamed up against another couple. With me, he was gentle and I was beginning to tell, very multi-layered.

Trent stayed at a comfortable distance, and Arinze disguised himself as much as possible so we could have uninterrupted fun. It almost went south when he went to get me a drink. Some guy started making advances. I tried to get him to leave me alone by ignoring him. That did not sit well with the guy. Next thing I knew; he was calling me out my name.

Until I heard his growl, I didn't know that Arinze had heard him too. It took me and Trent to calm him down. I didn't need my honor defended—not at the expense of his career. It wasn't worth it, especially over some college kid.

After leaving the rink, neither of us was ready to leave the other's presence, so we ordered take-out and drove to his condo in Santa Monica. We had dinner before deciding to take a stroll along the beach. Currently, we were seated in comfortable silence, looking out into the ocean. Small waves crashed the shoreline, carrying the salty smell I could feel dancing on my taste buds. I sighed at the relaxing feel of my toes digging in the sand. The sun had begun to set, giving the horizon an orange reddish hue.

"I miss home sometimes," I blurted out.

"Home is where you make it. But I understand. I live thousands of miles away from mine." His tone was distant.

"From what you told me, your parents wanted better opportunities for you. So, your leaving is understandable." I sighed. "I left because I couldn't bear to stay."

My eyes remained fixed on the rolling waves, but the intensity of Arinze's gaze burned my temple. All day he'd been so patient. Not once did he bring up the reason why we were in L.A. Or my parents. I tried to explain earlier, but he shut it down with a command to enjoy myself. I rarely talked about my parents, but I owed him an explanation.

"I grew up in the public's eye. The only child to Raymond and

Anita Bowman. Dad was a top, Black studio exec while mom was a famous costume designer. I wanted for nothing, but that came at a price. I was always the center of unwanted attention from the press. Being Black came with extra scrutiny in these circles. They couldn't wait until I screwed up.

They got what they wanted when I was seventeen. My parents' marriage went through a rough patch. The media had a field day reporting on their alleged affairs. I thought I knew my parents, so I didn't let it bother me at first. They'd printed lies before."

I took in a long breath before exhaling slowly. "One day, I heard them yelling at each other. Explaining that the affairs they had weren't physical but emotional. I didn't know what that meant until they started talking about the marriage not being what they promised each other when they got married. Apparently, they agreed not to have kids—just pursue their careers until I came along."

I rubbed my forehead. I've wished so many times I didn't go looking for my homework in the study that night. That night changed everything for me. My chest constricted at the thought that the people I loved most in the world didn't really want me.

"Jas…"

I held up my hand silencing him. I didn't want pity. That wasn't my intent. "I dropped my homework binder, so they heard me." I shrugged. "I won't bore you with their attempts to tell me they didn't mean what they said. Over the next several months, they went to couples' therapy, then we did family therapy. All to fix our family and I still couldn't let it go. So, I spent less and less time with them. I stayed in my room most of the time and couldn't wait to go off to college and leave them behind." I scoffed at myself. "I lived every day as though they would always be there." A tear rolled down my cheek.

"How did they die?" Arinze rubbed my back.

"One of the films my mom worked on got nominated for

something in Cannes. We were all supposed to go. You know, use it as a mini vacation. I bailed last minute. Went to my friend Aubree's party. They died in a plane crash on their way back."

The day Aubree's mom called me down to breakfast, and I saw Aunty Delia was the worst day of my life. My mind refused to wrap around what they were telling me. I moved in with Aunty Delia immediately. I had my cousins, but I vowed then to have a big family of my own someday. I wanted my child to have siblings they could do life with.

My parents had money set aside for me, but they had a lot of debt that had to be paid. Bad investments in movies and other things. Our family house was sold to offset the debt. I couldn't live there even if I wanted to. I finished college in L.A then moved to Chicago a few years later.

We sat in comfortable silence for a few moments before Arinze pulled me into his lap. He got me to straddle him. I lowered my eyes, but he lifted my head with his index finger. He pulled me closer until our foreheads touched, his arms securing me in place.

"I'm sorry you went through that. Now Ella makes so much more sense."

I gave him a faint chuckle.

"Close your eyes."

I raised my brow, but did as I was instructed. Still with his forehead against mine, he said, "Allow your mind to relax. Focus on the sounds of the waves. Deep long breath in, slow exhale."

It was so hard with him so close to me. His good looks weren't up for debate. Sexier than that though was the way he protected and nurtured me. Centering my mind, I filled my lungs to capacity and slowly let it out. We both did the exercise three more times. Seconds later, I heard his raspy voice envelope me.

"I'm so glad your journey led you to my path. But physical movement without shifting perspective will still have you bound, baby."

He moved his hand up my neck, threading his fingers through my hair. "Your parents loved you. They wouldn't have taken the time to fix whatever was broken if they didn't. Were you hard on them? Yeah. But you did what you knew to do as a teen. It's part of growing up. Don't reduce the time you had with your parents to that valley season y'all went through. Ask God for grace to push past and keep moving." He leaned back a little and stared into my eyes.

"What?"

"You do believe in God, right? I don't do that universe or atmosphere thing."

That made me chuckle and I swatted his shoulder. "Yes, I believe in God. The Creator of the universe."

"Ok, just checking."

He massaged my scalp a little before pulling me back to him, our foreheads once again making contact. The next thing out of his mouth was Psalm 23. I was not expecting this man to pray over me. When he was done, he cupped my face.

"The Lord is your Shepherd. It didn't say *a* shepherd. He's *yours*—to guide, restore, make sure you don't want for anything. I know it's been years, but the guilt seems to still tug at you. You can't work that out on your own. I'll help as much as you need me to, but I ain't Jesus."

I nodded, not trusting myself to speak. Arinze maneuvered us so that I was now seated between his legs with my head on his chest. We talked some more. He told me about his family. His dad had two brothers and there was a total of ten grandchildren, of which he was the first. I asked him about his cousin in the NBA and he acted like it was no big deal. I shared with him that my dad and I bonded over basketball. I guess I was the son he had but didn't know he wanted. With my mom, our thing was horseback riding. We used to ride for hours before taking our horses back to the stables we had behind the house.

Arinze gave me details on why he needed a fake girlfriend.

His grandmother sounded like a piece of work. I shared about my dream of the flower shop. I'd come to expect his words of encouragement and he didn't disappoint. Surprisingly, he knew the shopping complex as his niece had dance classes in a dance studio located in the same complex.

The rhythm of his heartbeat moved in sync with mine. It also provided the perfect backdrop for slumber and my eyelids started to cave. When he noticed I was sleeping, he asked if I wanted him to take me home. "Or..." he hesitated a bit, "you could use my guestroom."

I had done everything totally out of character already, so I texted my aunt that I'd be back in the morning. Minutes later, Arinze gave me a piggyback ride the short distance to the high rise where his condo was. After a brief tour, I took a shower and dressed in one of his tee shirts and shorts. I snuggled into the bed he showed me. Before he turned in, he made sure I was okay and didn't need anything.

At some time during the night, I jolted up from a bad dream. Reliving the death of my parents often had that effect. My lids were heavy as I tried to gain my bearings. Realizing where I was, I suddenly felt lonely and exposed. Getting out of bed, I made my way to the kitchen for a glass of water then made my way down the hall to Arinze's room. The door was slightly ajar. I entered and his eyes popped opened.

"What's wrong?" his gruff voice washed over me.

"Bad dream."

He stretched out his hand, motioning me forward. "Come here."

I got in the bed with him, and he pulled me close to his chest, his arms wrapped around me. "Relax."

I couldn't get my mind to settle. I barely knew this man, but the comfort his arms provided felt like home. Fear clawed through me. I could fall deeply in love with him. With love came loss. I'd lose my mind if I lost him. What did I look like, setting myself up for that kind of heartbreak? The potential of it was why I had stuck with Derrick all these years. I almost didn't make it when my parents died. The battle in my mind got more creative and vicious with possibilities.

He placed a light kiss on my temple. "I hear you thinking. Stop it."

The easiest way to stop it was to halt whatever this was in its tracks.

9

ARINZE

asmine must have lost her mind.

My eyes scanned through the email I'd received from Rent A Bae. For the umpteenth time in so many days, my vision was blurred with rage at the words that nearly sent me over the edge.

"*… we regret to inform you that your optimal match declined the assignment. We'll be sending you a replacement as soon as possible…*"

It'd been two weeks since I boarded a flight from L.A to Vancouver. I had to do some consulting work and promotion. I did a mental search to see if I had done anything wrong. That night she spent in my arms provided me peace I didn't know I was missing. I could breathe better with her coconut shampoo wafting up my nostrils. By the time I woke up, she was already showered and ready to go. I should've been more attentive to Jasmine's mood. Ciara was on me about my schedule and things I needed to take care of. I wanted to cook breakfast for her, but knew I couldn't, so I had my chef stop by.

We ate breakfast which she mostly moved around on the plate. I asked her what was wrong, but she told me nothing. I didn't believe her, but didn't want to badger her. I guessed she was thinking about what was happening between us. At a point, I was too. Especially when she kept silencing her ringing phone and clearing text messages.

During our talk on the beach, she asked about my shift after our kiss. I was honest about walking in on a heated conversation she was engaged in. She explained it was an ex, but at breakfast, seeing the name Derrick continuously pop up, I wasn't so sure. However, that didn't mean I didn't feel a vibe, and I knew she did too. I took her back home and was on to handle business. The next day I left L.A for Vancouver while she waited for Ella's MRI results. The news was favorable, and she was on a plane back to Atlanta two days later.

We'd talked constantly. After a long day on set, I went back to my hotel. My routine was the same. Shower, order dinner, talk to Jasmine, then I turned in. Her voice was like balm to my soul. The melodic sound of her laughter when I said something funny, or she laughed at her own jokes was now something I looked forward to hearing. Even her venting about another bride that didn't know what she wanted—I welcomed it all.

She also asked about my day, and I shared facts that, according to her, made her look at movies differently. I even got to talk to her friend, Aubree, once. Our connection was quick and deeper than I've had with anyone outside of my family.

Several days of constant contact, then I get this email. I called her immediately, but she was ghost. She'd blocked me from her social media, phone, and even email. The last few days on set were torture. I went from the initial shock to simmering anger. Where did I go wrong? Was she even okay? I had no idea where she stayed or her friend's number. But she told me where she worked.

It was Friday. I landed in Atlanta a few hours ago, and I was about to pull up at Jasmine's job. Anger coursed through my body. Yeah, she'd lost her mind, but I was about to help her find it. I lifted my eyes from typing a response to Cheta, who thought the situation was funny. My gaze met Sean's smirk through the rearview mirror.

"What?" I hit send on my text.

He chuckled. "You doing that thing you do with your jaw when you're angry."

"What you talking about, man?"

"Hmmm. We almost there. You need to get whatever has you about to act up together, before you go in."

I rolled my shoulders. "I'm good."

A few minutes later, Sean parked the car in front of Bloom Floral Design, and I got out. Before I closed the door, his low laughter sounded.

"I wanna meet this woman."

Waving him off, I strolled into the building. Walking up to the receptionist, I inquired about Jasmine. My emotions swung from worry and annoyance as she tapped some keys in her computer. Worry about Jasmine's well-being and annoyance with her actions. Once I was told Jasmine had gone out to lunch, anger became the dominate emotion. My teeth clenched when she told me that Jasmine would soon be back.

I was about to tell her that I'd wait when an elderly woman came from around the corner. She could pass for the late Betty White's twin. I knew immediately this was the woman Jasmine complained about. Her boss. She acknowledged me briefly and gave the receptionist instructions. As she turned to leave, she paused and looked at me. Her eyes widened.

"Oh, my good Lord. You're that actor. The one in the action war film, *The Great Defense.* My Stanley loves that movie."

With the possessive she put in front of the name, and the way her eyes sparkled, I assumed Stanley to be her husband or someone special. She looked to be in her mid-fifties. I loved when I saw mature couples still so enamored with each other. That's how my grandparents were as well. I smiled and nodded in acknowledgement. A gnawing feeling of betrayal pricked my heart. Jasmine didn't like this woman. I shouldn't either.

Nze, get it together. How can you be loyal to someone who wants nothing to do with you?

"Have you been helped? Are you getting married? Who's the lucky lady?" She rattled off questions.

I opened my mouth to respond when she waved her hands franticly. "Hold on. Would you mind signing an autograph for my Stanley?"

I nodded. "It'll be my pleasure."

She scurried back to where she came out from while I took a seat in the corner of the lobby. I pulled out my phone. Before I could unlock it, I heard *her*.

I missed that sound. My eyes darted to the glass double doors. Excitement and anger increased my heart rate. The yearning to hear her voice, to hear that sound and her willfully denying me the pleasure unsettled me. Its potency lay in its ability to affect my mood. Right now, it pulled me apart at the seams. Almost tempting me to grovel at her feet for mercy. Asking for a chance to fix whatever I did wrong.

Almost.

Almost, because when her laughter faded, his appeared. It didn't matter who *he* was. Fury rippled through me. We weren't supposed to have significant others. Did she lie about that? I'd been miserable and she was chummy.

They entered the lobby area just as the older woman came from the back. I stood and Jasmine turned her head with searching eyes toward my direction. My stomach settled, knowing that Jasmine felt my presence. Stepping out from the shadows, her eyes widened. The man she was with darted his eyes between the two of us, confusion clearly etched on his face.

Jasmine's boss walked up to me and handed me a small note-book to autograph. Smiling at her, I obliged her request. My eyes returned to Jasmine who seemed to regain her bearings.

"Umm, Derrick let me get your portfolio from my office. I'll be right back," Jasmine said.

She began heading to the back and her boss fell in step with her. I clenched my teeth and glanced over the guy I now knew as Derrick. The fact that this was the guy whose phone call she'd ignored several times in my condo further had me looking at her really funny.

Chantel's antics floated through my mind. I had ignored a lot of the signs. I had too much to lose to do that to myself a second time. If this was me taking a random woman to throw off my grandmother, I wouldn't even bother. But this was someone I knew I could care about deeply. In fact, while I was in Canada, I made up my mind that I wanted to pursue her. Now, I was having second thoughts as to whether she was worth it.

Jasmine came rushing back. Her eyes met mine and she walked over. Her closeness calmed but didn't quench my rage. Hands in my pockets, I stared down at her. She dipped her head, refusing to meet my eyes.

She whispered, "What are you doing here?"

"What time do you get off?" I asked, completely ignoring her question.

Her eyes darted around. "In three hours. But—"

"I'll be back then. Do not leave."

"But Ari—"

"Remember when you told me you thought airmen and sailors were more chill than the other branches of the military?" My voice was low, but crisp.

This time her eyes met mine, searching for an explanation.

"Don't try me, so I won't have to disprove your theory."

Her eyes widened and the dude she left standing cleared his throat. I glanced at Jasmine. Her eyes pleaded with me. This was her place of work. I'd never do anything to embarrass her or make things even more awkward with her boss. I strolled to the door but stopped when I got to dude who obviously needed some attention.

I turned to Jasmine. "Three hours. Also, you might wanna get your friend a cough drop. Something seems to be caught in his throat." Without a backward glance, I left.

~

With a crease in my forehead, I glanced over at Jasmine. She was seated in the front of my truck as I drove us to our destination.

"So, let me get this straight. You decided we weren't a good fit. You also made the decision to not talk to me about it. You were on such a roll that you then decided to block me from being able to reach you." I summarized the story Jasmine just told me.

Like I figured, Jasmine came out of her office at ten minutes before her closing time. Seated in my truck, I watched her glance around the parking lot before she scurried to her car. As she was about to enter her car, I came out of mine. If I wasn't so annoyed, the look on her face would've been comical.

I asked Sean to drive her car and had her get into my truck with me. We were headed to a popular restaurant I frequented in downtown Atlanta. Not only was the ambience great, but the food was fantastic, and it afforded me the privacy I needed. I'd been going there since my Morehouse days, so I knew the owners very well.

"Yes, and stop looking at me like that!"

"How am I looking at you?"

She cut her eyes at me. "Like I'm stupid."

A smile danced around my lips at her outburst. "I'm questioning your decision-making skills. But I don't think you're stupid."

She scowled.

I chuckled. "Now, I do think you're a coward. And I must confess I'm surprised."

She sucked her teeth. "So, because I don't want to be matched with you, I'm a coward?" She turned in her seat, arms folded across her chest.

"No, I think you're a coward because I know you don't even believe what you just said. Even if you did, instead of talking to me, you had me blocked. That's very telling."

"Whatever. I've heard about you Nigerian men. Very domineering."

I stilled. My grip on the steering wheel tightened. I hated when people did that. Use the experience of a few to judge the collective. Those would be the same people that cried foul when it was done to them. I liked Jasmine, so I was about to nip this in the bud.

"We're not doing that." The iciness in my voice was intentional.

"What?"

"Making blanket generalizations like the one you just made. We deal with each other based off our experience with *each* other. There are some characterizations I could make about you, but it would be unfair to place you in a particular category because of my experience with a few. Besides you can find a domineering man anywhere in the world. It's a man thing."

She sighed. "You're right. I'm sorry."

"Accepted. So, about this guy, Derrick..."

"Derrick is a friend who...wait. Why are you questioning me?" She let out a labored breath. "Look Arinze, I know what I said before and I thought I could do it, but I realized we're not as compatible as the artificial intelligence said we are."

I remained silent. Her defensiveness let me know that her resistance was rooted in something deeper. I wasn't in the habit of chasing women that didn't want to be caught. I had to receive the same energy I was giving, or there was no point. It's that simple for me. I wasn't going to push her. More than anything, I needed her to be comfortable. If she thought, she couldn't do it then it is what it is. I knew she was expecting an argument, but I wasn't going to give her one. I simply nodded my head.

"Okay." Turning into the restaurant, I parked in my usual spot at the back. "You still wanna grab something to eat? Sean is behind us. You can leave if that's what you wanna do."

She cleared her throat. "Ummm…I can eat."

"Bet."

My ringtone broke the air of awkwardness between us. It was Vivienne. She'd been trying to reach me for some days, but I hadn't been able to call back. I climbed out of the car and answered as I walked around to help Jasmine out.

"Hey Viv, can I call you back a little later? You good?"

"I'm fine. How are you so difficult to pin down? Call me back. It's about the gala."

I'd completely forgotten that I agreed to be her plus one some months back. I could feel Jasmine's eyes on me so I told Vivienne I would get with her later and disconnected the call. I threw the keys to Sean, took Jasmine's hand, and proceeded to the back entrance. As we rode the elevator up, Jasmine had her eyes on me, so I gave her mine.

"You got something you wanna ask me, Jas? I hear you thinking."

She rolled her eyes. "Don't act like you know me."

"I don't. I'm trying to, but you don't want that." I shrugged.

The elevator stopped and I grabbed Jasmine's hand and led her through the kitchen. Ma Bess approached with a smile once she laid eyes on me. After she scolded me for not coming to see her for three months, I introduced her to Jasmine. She gave me an excited look at which I shook my head. She, like all the other women in my life, hounded me about settling down. She ushered us to my normal booth. After handing us menus, she took our drink orders, and told us she would be right back.

After settling Jasmine in, I sat opposite her. Glancing down at the menu, I said, "I think you should try the—"

"Okay fine...who is Vivienne?" Jasmine leaned back in her seat and crossed her arms over her chest.

The action pushed up her cleavage. Before getting lost in her allure, I lifted my eyes to her face. My expression, aplomb. "A friend."

"With benefits?"

I shrugged. "Whatever the occasion calls for."

"So why can't she go with you to Nigeria?"

"I didn't want to blur lines, but since you declined, she's now an option." The waiter brought over our drinks, pausing my speech. Once he left, I continued. "I'm not in the mood to get to know someone else so..."

An emotion danced behind her eyes. I wasn't really sure what it was, but I didn't ask. After suggesting what she should have and placing our orders, we began to talk. Over the course of the meal, the feeling of comfort and familiarity returned. We laughed, joked, and caught up on the week she cut me off.

I wanted her to try the apple pie I'd fallen in love with over the years. She agreed only if I would share it with her, which I did. Soon after, we were back in the parking lot behind the restaurant. I walked her to her car, but I felt her hesitate to get in.

"You okay?" I steadied my hands in my pockets and leaned into her.

"I'll do it."

"And what might that be?" I knew what she was talking about, but for almost running me insane with worry and anger, I was going to let her tell me.

"Be your pretend girl."

I lifted my brows. "What changed your mind?" I stepped closer, trapping her between my body and the car. Recognition flashed through her eyes when she figured I was taunting her.

She straightened her spine and nudged me away. "Move, Nze."

I chuckled, stepping back a bit. "Is that enough space for your confessions?"

"I'm not confessing anything. I thought about it. You leave in two weeks and since you helped me out with Ella, the least I can do is return the favor." She tucked a loose tress behind her ear. "Making you take someone you don't want to, or you going through the vetting process again isn't fair."

I saw straight through her story, but I was gonna let her make it. Anything to have her with me. Instead of calling her out, I put my hand on my chest. "How kind of you, Ms. Bowman. Thank you."

She bowed her head and giggled. "You're welcome. Besides, it would be hard finding someone like me."

"Like you, huh? Confident. My kind of pretend woman." I winked at her.

"There is one condition."

"Let's have it. If it's agreeable, why not?"

"When we get back, we are done. That's it."

The thought of that possibility made my heart skip a beat. "What if I don't want to be done?"

She shook her head and shrugged. "That's the only way this is happening."

It was getting late, and she had two weddings to work the next day, so I had to get her home. Therefore, I acquiesced, but not before I gave her conditions of my own.

"Agreed, but two things."

"I'm listening."

"You have to be all in." I paused for a second. "And...you can never lie to me."

She frowned. "I'm insulted. Why would I lie?"

I smirked. "Not my intention to offend." I lifted her face with my index finger. "Do we have a deal?"

"No sex. But I agree to everything else."

I leaned into her. Her breath hitched. Her reaction to my closeness did something to my ego. I cupped her face. Desire danced in her eyes. I pressed my lips against hers. Lush, just as I remembered. I slid my tongue past the barrier of her lips, teasing hers to tango. When it was evident we needed to breathe, we broke contact.

"Baby, when I *do* explore your body," I said against her lips, "there won't be anything pretend about it." I leaned my forehead against hers. That gesture had somehow become our thing.

I heard her swallow and my other head stirred. It was time for me to go. I unlocked her door and helped her in. Once she was in safely, I had her lower the window.

"Text me when you get in. Don't make me come look for you, Jasmine."

She laughed. I stepped back and she drove away. I walked the short distance to my car and got in.

"You got it bad," Sean said.

"I got something. Whether it's good or bad is yet to be determined."

JASMINE

ealousy made me do it.

She might've known him before me, but there was no way I was letting Vivienne enjoy an advantage I knew he'd offered me first.

That was what my mind told my heart when Arinze mentioned having his "friend" be my replacement. I didn't admit the thought to Aubree when I told her I'd changed my mind about going. Ever since I told her it was Arinze or Mr. Butterscotch, as we called him, who I was matched with, she'd been #TeamArinze. Instead of coming clean with my friend, I told her I felt bad for failing him.

It was Wednesday morning and I was flying across the ocean to the continent. Lifting my eyes from my Kindle, I took in a sleeping Arinze across from me on their family jet. The light pressure he applied to my healing sprained ankle that was still in his lap probably meant he wasn't fully asleep. I had no business running in heels to the van to get an extra floral arrangement for a last-minute wedding party addition.

Since he couldn't see me, I could really ogle him. He wore an army green tee that showcased his ripped physique over some navy-blue joggers. They were from ZF again. He told me that stood for Zeidu Fashions. They were designers out of West Africa. He had sandals on his well-groomed feet. His butterscotch skin was well moisturized, not an ash in sight. The hands he used to absently massage my ankle were strong with nails that were cut short and pristine. While I was braiding my hair the day before, he had his barber over at his house. Whoever he was, did a good job.

Since meeting Arinze, I'd seen plenty pictures of him on the internet. I'd even watched a few interviews he'd done. Watched only one movie, as war action films weren't my thing. He was always so well put together. Yet, when he was with me or his family, he was so different. Simple. He thrived on making sure everyone else was okay. Our phone calls always ended with him asking if I needed anything. I usually didn't, but the fact he asked and genuinely waited until I convinced him I didn't, weakened, enamored, and scared me at the same time.

The chemistry between us had been established way before we reconnected. After L.A and sleeping in his arms, I knew I had to run. Self-preservation was the only thing on my mind when I blocked him and declined the assignment. Looking at Arinze now and the funny thing my heart was doing, my perceived advantage over Vivienne was beginning to feel like set up for heartbreak.

Two weeks had gone by since I decided to take this leap and I was trying not to "dress rehearsal tragedy" as Aubree often said I do. In that time, Arinze had been in and out of Atlanta with work, but he never failed to keep in touch. When he was in Atlanta, he took me out on dates. Sometimes he picked the places or sometimes I did. He claimed Atlanta as his city, so I tried to leave it up to him most of the time.

Last weekend, I got to meet his cousins. Arinze told me about Jidenna's late wife. I recognized the grief in his eyes almost immediately. It mirrored mine, but somewhere behind them also lay mystery. His little girl was so adorable it made no sense. She had all her uncles wrapped around her little finger.

Cheta was late to lunch that day, but the second he entered, I was star struck. Unlike Arinze, Cheta was more boisterous and friendly, just as I thought he would be from watching him play basketball on television. He took over the room when he entered. He deliberately got on Arinze's nerves by hugging me or placing his hand at the small of my back. The way Arinze's face contorted was comical and reminded me of the day he met Derrick in my office.

Thinking of Derrick, it was funny how he was suddenly able to find the time to see me. I was positive he'd talked to Aunty Delia, and she told my business. I knew she meant well, but Derrick's questions were annoying, seeing as though I'd already let him know we were done.

I didn't tell Arinze the extent of our relationship because I didn't want him to judge me. I'd concluded and accepted that I cared what he thought of me. How could I share that I hadn't loved myself enough to know I was worth more than the way I allowed Derrick to treat me. It was one thing not to want love. It was a whole other thing to allow someone who claimed to love me to treat me like an afterthought.

The cabin was quiet except for the hum and occasional roar of the engine. I was the only one awake. Cheta was toward the front of the plane asleep with his headset on while Jidenna and Uju occupied the back bedroom. Swiping my finger across the screen, I woke up my sleeping Kindle. Based on the time, we'd been flying for four hours.

Yesterday, even with two people working on my head, it seemed like it took forever to get these box braids in. I got home so late. Thank God that as she always does, my bestie was there to help me pack. By the time I slipped between my sheets, it was time to wake up. Arinze loved to tease me about being late, so I was determined to prove him wrong. When the fellas arrived to pick me up, I was on time, but dragging.

My eyes lit up when I saw that Arinze had coffee for me. Shortly after we took off, the crew served breakfast. With a full belly and barely enough sleep, I succumbed to my drooping lids.

Now I was wide eyed looking at everyone sleep. A pinch from my bladder reminded me that I needed to use the restroom. I placed my Kindle on the seat next to me and started to gently remove my foot from Arinze's lap. He grabbed it and peered open his eyes.

"Where you going?"

I smiled at him. "Welcome back. Can I go to the restroom?"

He grinned, releasing my leg. "You good?"

"Yeah. Woke up not too long ago. That shut eye was needed."

"Good, but try and stay awake 'cause by the time we get there, it'll be nighttime. I don't want you to have a hard time sleeping."

This is what I'm talking about. He cares about the littlest things that concern me. "Got it." I stood, leaned over to rub his bald head, and placed a kiss on it.

"Be right back. I wanna go over the members of the Kalu family again. Make sure I got everything." I turned to walk away, but he grabbed my hand.

"We gonna have to do something about you not following instructions."

My brows came together, waiting for him to elaborate.

"What did I tell you about that head kiss?"

I shook my head. "To follow it up with a real kiss."

Arinze inclined his head and I bent and brushed my lips gently against his. Before I could break free, his hand went to the back of my neck, holding me in place. Warmth surged through me as I granted his tongue entry into my mouth. A thorough sweep elicited a moan that quickly brought me to my senses. I broke our connection.

Using my thumb to wipe the gloss from his lips, I met his hooded eyes. "You're going to make me wake up these folks."

Giving me a half shrug, he asked, "So? For the next two weeks, you're mine, remember?"

"Will you let me forget?"

"Absolutely not. Go handle your business. Let me get us something to eat."

After relieving myself, I washed my hands and then dabbed a damp paper towel over my face. I headed back to my seat. I admired the eight-seater jet, something I didn't have time to do before. I'd teased him about being all fancy with a private jet. He explained it belonged to all three of them. I arrived at my seat just as the hostess was leaving. She gave me a polite smile which I returned. Arinze removed the dome plate covers on the food she had brought.

"What did you get?"

"We'll definitely have dinner when we land, so I figured something light."

My stomach rumbled as the aroma from the crispy, golden brown crab cakes, sweet potatoes wedges and sautéed lemony asparagus wafted up my nostrils.

"This is great."

"There's dessert. Just say the word."

"Thank you. I'm starving."

We said grace and I attacked my food. I was starving, but I also had no idea what the family dinner would consist of, so the plan was to be full of what I could recognize and pronounce. We ate in comfortable silence. Every so often we discussed something random, then went back to eating. Soon after, we were done and set our trays aside. Arinze picked up my feet and eased my sandals off.

"How does your ankle feel?"

I chuckled. "If you want my feet on you just say that. I sprained it last weekend. It's much better."

Smirking, he swallowed his rebuttal and continued to massage my ankle.

"Okay, so let me see if I have this right—"

"Relax Jas, introductions will be made. You don't have to memorize anything."

"I know, but I'd like to be sure I got it." I took a breath, trying to recall what he told me a few days ago. Suddenly my eyes widened. "We never discussed what our origin story is."

"Now you're just trying to bruise my ego."

I laughed. "What are you talking about?"

"You don't know our origin story?"

"I mean, I know how we met, but is that what you wanna go with?"

"Why weave a tale when the truth is so beautiful?" He winked at me.

I felt my cheeks heat up. I closed my eyes and shook my head, mentally discarding all the illicit images that formed in my mind. He chuckled, and I rolled my eyes.

"You think it's funny?" I asked.

"It's hilarious, watching you squirm like that." He let up the armrest and patted the seat next to him. "Come here."

"No, Nze, I'm serious. I wanna get this together."

"Come here, Jas."

Sighing, I moved to the seat closer to him. He pulled me closer 'til my back was leaned partially against his chest. He draped his muscular arm across my body, securing me in place. He kissed the back of my ear causing shivers to creep up my spine.

"Nze..."

"I love the way you say my name," he whispered. "You know this is not an exam. All you have to do is be your sexy self and look at me like you can't breathe without me."

I chuckled. "Really?"

"Yep, the first one you already got. My mission is to work on getting you to the second… for real."

"Arinze, we said—"

"I know what you said…" He peppered kisses along my neck. "The woman's right to change her mind is a powerful concept, and I intend to help you do just that."

I wasn't going to win this argument now. How could I when having him so close to me was scrambling my brain cells? I ignored him and cleared my throat instead.

"Back to the topic at hand. Your grandparents had three boys. First, your dad, then Cheta's, then Jidenna's."

His fingers caressed my side. "Correct."

"You have three younger sisters. The oldest of them is Adaugo, who's the one getting married. She and her fiancé live in Canada. If…." I held up my index finger, stopping him from helping me. A sigh escaped my lips when I couldn't remember. "What's her name?"

He kissed my hair. "Ifunanya. You can call her Ify. She recently returned to Enugu after completing her masters. She works for Kalu International. Then Chioma, the baby."

I smiled. The way he talked about the women in his life gave me more insight into who he was. "Right. Cheta has two older sisters. He's the baby and Jidenna has two sisters. He's in the middle."

He squeezed me tight. "Bravo."

"Remind me how to greet older people."

"*Ndewo*. But you can greet in English. They'll understand."

I sat up and faced him. "I know, but I want to. If this was real, I'd want to embrace your culture. Without forgetting mine, of course."

His lips turned up in a smile. "Is that right?" He draped my leg over his knee.

I raised my brow. "Let me find out you're a leg man."

"Nah, I'm an all over your body man. Since I can't get that, I'm working with what I can get." He winked, then placed his gaze on my soft pink painted toes. "I like this color against your caramel skin."

Trying my best to ignore the tingling in my body, I redirected us. "You're going to have to enunciate the names for me. I know I'll mess some up."

"It's not the end of the world. Look, I don't want you flustered about anything." He gave me a pointed look; I guess needing me to agree, so I nodded.

"I'm glad you wanna learn, but I don't want you stressing over it. Even my mom had a hard time enunciating some names correctly."

I frowned. "Your mom isn't Nigerian?"

"She is, but she's Yoruba. An ethnic group from the western part of Nigeria." He shrugged. "My family is Igbo, so some names she had trouble pronouncing correctly at first."

When he said that, it reminded me of so many things I wanted to ask. I hated to sound ignorant, but I didn't expose myself to a lot about the continent. I knew the basics, but nothing too deep. Aubree teased me the other day that I didn't know any Nigerians.

"I mean everyone knows someone from Nigeria or knows someone that knows someone," she'd said. "They're everywhere."

"Is that all you got?"

I picked up my Sprite and took a sip. "So, I was on the internet…"

He leaned his head on the headrest and let out a dramatic sigh. "Oh boy. What did they say I did?"

"Not you, silly. I read some things about Africans."

He furrowed his brows.

"No, I know you're not the collective, but I wanna ask for insight."

"Okay, wassup?"

"I read about polygamy—that almost every man has more than one wife." I twirled one of my braids.

"As you said, I don't speak for over a billion people that live in Africa or the two hundred million that live in Nigeria. I can only speak for myself and my world view." He took a breath, then continued. "Yes, polygamy is a thing. Neither my grandfather, father, uncles, myself, or my cousins are interested in polygamy. Do I have friends who grew up in polygamous households? Yes. Did I? No.

"It's the same way you have Black American men who have multiple children by different women. No rhyme or reason. But then you also have Black American men like my friend DJ—you know from the wedding—and a whole lot of other guys I roll with who are faithful to their wives and love them more than themselves."

When he spoke, my mind immediately went to those celebrities having kids like it's going out of style. Then there's Aubree and Rich who make love look so beautiful. "You have a point. I get that." I took another sip. "Okay, what about the notion that Africans don't want Black Americans there?"

"Who told you that? I've heard it before and I'm yet to see one viral video of a Black American going to any country in Africa and people telling them they're not wanted. Truth be told, my countryman will treat a foreigner better than me sometimes."

He snickered. "I remember when DJ came home with me. Everywhere we went, it was like he walked on water. I've also heard that Africans think they're better. I don't know about all Africans, but Nigerians are the proudest people I know. We think we're better than each other. So, it's not personal. We're raised to be competitive, strive for the absolute best and take no prisoners while we are doing it." He paused.

"Get this…in school, at the end of a semester or any competition, if you come in second, the typical Nigerian parent won't say they're proud or 'well done'." He thumbed his nose. "Instead, they'd ask if the person that came in first place had two heads or if they were better. You know what that does?"

I figured he didn't really need an answer this time, so I stayed silent.

"It makes you more competitive. To gain their approval. We're not better than any human. We just know that we better be the best at whatever we do, and we believe that with all we got."

Arinze set my feet on the floor and scooted to the edge of his seat. His forearms where on his knees as he leaned forward. I could see the creases on his forehead. There was a shift in the air around us. I almost hated that I asked anything. I was about to change the topic when he raised his index finger.

"Oh, I got one…Africans call Black Americans names. Well, Black Americans call us names as well. I didn't know I was an African booty scratcher until I overheard my college roommate refer to me as one. Also didn't know that being African meant that I was automatically the measuring unit for anything that was nasty or unkempt until someone said it to me as a joke. I was raised a proud Igbo man. But I don't take what one ignorant person said about me as the Black American collective thought. My best friend is Black American." He bent his head. His octave had gone from cool and calm to fiery and passionate in a few seconds flat.

"I'm sorry," I whispered.

He turned to me. "Come here."

I moved to his lap. His arms snaked around my waist, holding me close. He placed his head on my chest.

"There's nothing to be sorry for. You didn't do anything. As a Nigerian celebrity in America whose audience is mainly Black American, I'm asked these kinds of questions often. It was worse in the early days of my career. On almost every promo tour I did, I found myself defending and or explaining a collection of people. It gets tiring. I'm sorry for raising my voice."

I caressed his head. I noticed it calmed him and was now one of my favorite things to do. "I can understand that."

"We're all products of our experiences. We're not monolithic, nor will we be great in Africa or in the Diaspora if we can't rise above. Just like there's a difference between an exposed Black American who has lived overseas or has educated themselves on the world outside America, there's also a difference when it comes to Africans.

"You have those who were born abroad, but have never been home. Those born abroad who've lived in both places or who came over at an early age. Then finally, those who migrated abroad at an older age. Nothing wrong with any of these groups, but our mindsets and perspectives will differ, so we can't be grouped together."

I palmed his head in my hands and brushed my lips against his. "Agreed."

"With that said, going forward, no generalizations, please. Anything you wanna know about me, ask, and I promise I'll tell you. I told you when you agreed to do this for me, you're good with me. Trust me."

Arinze gripped my chin and drew my face to his. He brushed his lips against mine, giving me a few pecks, then he deepened the kiss. My arms circled his neck as his hands gently massaged my back. Coming up for air, Arinze broke contact and reclined the seat into a bed. I tried to get up to move to my seat, but his grip tightened. "Nah, stay. I need to feel you on me."

My head tried to warn me against blurring the lines of reality. Our attraction was never the issue. Allowing myself to believe I could afford for it to become something more, was. Right now, my heart begged me to just be, so I did what I was told and got comfortable.

11

JASMINE

I can do this. Yes, I can do this.

I looked at my phone again, rereading Aubree's message.

Bree Breezy: You got this. Match energy. Remember, not all of them are gonna like you but I trust Arinze won't let anyone come at you sideways.

I placed the phone on the dresser and checked myself out again. The casual, green, O-neck dress with a black and white print at the bottom fit my curves perfectly. It was formal enough to meet a man's family for the first time, but comfortable enough for me to feel good in. I put on my diamond studs, opting not to put on any neckwear. I did a light beat on my face earlier and placed my mid-back length braids in a neat bun. Stepping back, I smoothed down the knee-length dress. I walked over to the bed and sat to put on the silver strappy heels I'd bought for this outfit.

I had no idea what to expect when we arrived several hours ago. But what I did see wasn't it. Arinze kept referring to where his family lived as a compound. This wasn't a compound; it was an estate. A massive one at that. When Arinze's driver met us at the airport and drove us through the humongous black gate, I was in total awe. As we drove up the driveway lined with palm trees, I stared out the window while Arinze pointed out which house belonged to who.

His parents, Cheta's and Jidenna's all had large, red brick bungalows with an ample amount of space between them. His grandparents' home was smaller and was a little further down. The grounds were well manicured, with different flowers, statues, and fountains. I didn't believe anything else could fit in this space. But then we drove about five more minutes and there was another set of houses. Three mansions to be exact, belonging to Arinze, Cheta, and Jidenna.

We dropped his cousins off and headed to his home. According to Arinze, no one knew we would arrive this early, so it gave us time to rest before dinner. When we got in, he gave me a brief tour of the two-story home. When I walked in, I did a double take. Again, I had no idea what to expect, but this wasn't it. If I wasn't sure I had landed in Nigeria, I'd think I was still in America. Well, except for the noise of the generator roaring behind the house. I found out it was absolutely necessary for survival with the unstable electricity in the country.

On the ground floor was a state-of-the-art kitchen, a spacious living room, a gym, a twelve-seater dining area, a study, and a movie theatre. I smiled when I saw the theatre had the poster of all the movies he'd acted in. There was also a bedroom and powder room. Upstairs were the other bedrooms including the master. I looked around this room I was in. It was one of six bedrooms in the house. Like the rest of the home, it had an African bohemian feel with ethnic art hanging on the walls. From what I saw, the heavy security presence at the entrance of the gate was necessary.

After having a soul rejuvenating shower, I climbed atop the king-sized bed and almost sunk in. I should've been able to sleep, but the nervousness in the pit of my stomach prevented such luxury. I did rest, until Arinze asked me to get ready for dinner at his grandparents' house.

With my sandal straps secured, I walked back to the mirror. I gave myself another pep talk. Then I thought of my flower shop. The reason I put myself in this situation.

"You look beautiful, baby."

I jumped at the sound of his voice. I turned to find Arinze leaned against the door frame. My eyes took inventory of this fine specimen of God's creation. He'd transformed from Arinze the American to Arinze the Nigerian. He had on a brown and white, short-sleeved African print set. On his feet were a simple pair of leather sandals.

"Thank you. You transform nice."

He sauntered over to me. "You approve?"

His cologne sent my senses into a frenzy, temporarily rendering me speechless. I nodded.

"You ready?"

"As ready as I'll ever be."

"You trust me?"

"Yes."

"Everything will be fine." Arinze took my hand and led me out of the room.

Minutes later, we walked up to the mid-sized home. The knots in my stomach still refused to settle. Arinze squeezed my hand; his reassuring smile did nothing for my nerves. Before he could knock on the door, it opened, and two young women flew to him.

"Brother Nze!" they shouted.

"Mama, *broda* is here!" someone else yelled from inside.

I stepped to the side and admired the display before me. Arinze's arms went around the ladies, squeezing them tightly before letting them go.

"You people should let him come in," a woman admonished.

Their eyes finally landed on me. Arinze took my hand, and

the two ladies stepped to the side to allow us entry. I could see the curiosity dancing in their eyes as their eyes darted between us. A woman met us in the foyer and immediately, I knew this was his mother. The picture he'd showed me didn't do her justice. Her dark skin glowed against the yellow flowing dress she had on. Her hair was black with some silver tresses. The women oozed money and class.

"*Omo mi.*" Her voice was so soft.

Arinze bent at the waist with "Ẹ kú alẹ́."

She answered, placing her hand on his back. When he stood, he pulled her into a hug. After releasing her, he reached for me.

"Mummy, this is Jasmine, my lady."

I genuflected the way Arinze taught me. "Good evening, ma."

"Ah, ah. Good evening, my dear. How are you?" She was talking to me, but her eyes kept moving to Arinze.

"I'm fine, ma.

"*Lati igba wo?*" she asked Arinze.

Arinze frowned. "Mummy, English. We met last year."

I wondered whether what she asked was what he responded to because I could sense some skepticism in her vibe. But then, she either liked me or didn't want to anger her son because the next thing I knew, she was tugging me along with her. Arinze followed.

She pulled me into the family room. I was relieved when Cheta and Jidenna shouted my name. That seemed to give me some validity. Uju ran up to me for a hug. Arinze's mom introduced me to his grandparents. His grandfather seemed happy, but his grandmother sized me up and didn't say much. Next, I met his father, uncles, and their wives. The two ladies that met us at the door were Arinze's younger sisters. The one that shouted for them to allow us to enter, I found out, was the bride. It was obvious Arinze got his complexion from his dad because his sisters were chocolate beauties just like his mom. Cheta and Jidenna's sisters would be arriving within the week.

Arinze's sisters quickly kidnapped me and took me to another part of the house. His baby sister was the chief interviewer. The bride had to caution her many times when she thought she went too far with the questions. The middle sister did more observing than questioning. By the time Arinze came to my rescue, I knew more about each one of them.

I had asked if there was anything I could help with for dinner. By the time we sat down to eat, I knew why they laughed me off. After we all sat down, house staff poured out seemingly from nowhere, setting the table, bringing food and drinks from the kitchen. Arinze explained every dish. There were various types of rice, stews, soups, fufu, plantains, snails, moi-moi, various types of fried meat, and chicken. After grace was said, everyone dug in. I chose rice and chicken. It was the safest bet for me. Arinze had fufu and some kind of soup. The aroma was divine.

"What's that?" I whispered to him.

"It's called onugbu soup. The English name is bitter leaf soup."

"So, it's bitter?"

"It's his favorite soup, so you have to know how to cook it well," his grandmother said from across the other end of the table. "I hope you will learn how to make it for him."

"Mama!" Arinze said.

A chilling silence fell across the room. I squeezed his thigh under the table. She hadn't been totally cold, but she hadn't been welcoming either. The rest might not trust me, but they didn't show it. His grandmother, on the other hand, didn't have a problem showing it. There was no need to spar with the woman. Underneath her ice, I knew she only wanted what was best for her grandson. Her husband gave her a disapproving look.

"If he tells me he wants it, of course I'll learn," I answered.

She grunted and everyone resumed eating. After dinner, the dishes were cleared, and we reconvened back in the family room. Arinze's grandpa started giving me a little history lesson on the town. From the conversation, I found out that both he and his wife were retired teachers. They sent their three boys to school in America. After their degrees, they came back home to start their company.

Sometime during the evening, Arinze excused himself to talk to his grandmother. She kept looking my way as they talked. Soon after, he hugged her, and she laughed. I guess all was well now. Arinze noticed the yawn I was trying to hide. He grabbed my hand and leaned over to me.

"Let's go."

"Are you sure? I'm fine."

"No, you're not. I need to get you to bed."

Not willing to argue any further, I allowed him to pull me up. We said our goodbyes. His sisters were arranging to come to his house in the morning, but he shut it down. He told them he would call when we were up. As we got to the door, a young lady came rushing in. She stopped before us. I took her in. She was beautiful with a figure to die for. She looked to be in her mid-twenties.

"Good evening, Arinze, I didn't know you were around. It was someone in town that told me they saw your car."

"And you are?" Arinze asked, his jaw clenched.

I had to do a double take because his tone dripped ice. I didn't know this man. He was always so tempered in tone. Even when he was irritated. The woman looked at me, then her eyes went to our joined hands. Her eyes met mine again and she rolled them. I raised a brow, but decided she wasn't a threat to me in any way.

"My name is Esther. My grandmother and yours are friends," she said.

Ah. This must be the woman in the video Arinze told me about. Before he could respond to her, Cheta appeared.

"Nze, I got this." He moved the girl, who seemed puzzled, to the side, and we continued on.

"Jazzy Jas." I turned to Cheta, smiling at the nickname he'd given me. "Welcome to the Motherland."

"Thanks! Goodnight, CK," I threw over my shoulder.

Once we were in the car, I turned to Arinze. "Are you okay?"

"Yeah."

"Was that her?"

He grunted. I laughed.

"It's funny to you?" He cut his eyes at me.

"Of course, it is. I'm literally saving your behind." I dusted off my shoulder. "As a matter of fact, we might have to renegotiate my money."

"You know you'd do it for free. Stop playing with me." He brought my hand up to his lips and kissed it.

I giggled. If only he knew how true his statement was.

Sunlight streaming through the trees, horn honks in the distance, freshly cut grass and the steady hum of the generator were some of the sights, scents, and sounds I'd become accustomed to in Enugu. I didn't know if it was because the Kalu estate was tucked away, or if this really was how life was here, but there wasn't the sense of urgency I was used to. Everything was laid back and I was in heaven. It was my third day here and every day started the same.

Arinze and I met in his living room for prayer. He wasn't kidding when he told me he didn't joke with his relationship with God. Afterwards we enjoyed a breakfast his staff prepared. Depending on how hot it was, we ate on the deck or in the dining area. It was so easy to talk about any and everything with him.

By mid-morning, we headed to his parents' home. That was another masterpiece in architecture. His mother had become sweet on me. We went out a few times and she loved being flanked by Adaugo on her right and me on her left. From what his sisters told me, she's glad Arinze was considering settling down.

His sisters and I got along great. They welcomed me and genuinely wanted to include me in the wedding preparations. I got to meet the event planner for the wedding and Adaugo kept wanting my input about the floral design. I could tell the planner was irritated, but I gave my candid opinion on small changes I thought would be nice.

After spending time with them, Arinze would whisk me off into the town. That man sure knew how to show a girl a good time. We'd gone golfing, been on an excursion through one of the many caves in the town, taken a boat ride across Nike Lake, and visited the National Museum of Unity. I learned so much that stunned and fascinated me at the same time. I'd also eaten things I couldn't pronounce.

Although Arinze wanted me to be adventurous with my taste buds, he didn't allow me to indulge too much. We finished off every night with a romantic dinner and conversation. Those conversations often ended in some heavy petting but surprisingly, he pulled us down to earth just in time. I smiled, remembering last night when he abruptly ended our kiss. He smirked and I threw a pillow at him before stomping away.

Following me, he'd said, "Your rules, baby."

I slammed the door in his face. His laughter reverberated through the hallway as he continued on to his room. After taking a cold shower and dressing for bed, I noticed a glass of the hibiscus mint iced tea I'd come to love. I'd tasted the magenta-colored drink at his mom's house and fell in love. I picked up the note that was next to it.

Your bratty is cute but calm yourself down ~ Nze.

I'd chuckled, enjoyed my drink while chatting with Aubree. Later I sent him a text. He was right, no sex was my rule. I couldn't risk seeing him again, so I sent him a text.

Thank you. But I still don't like you.

The lies you tell

I sent a couple of laughing emojis, then

Goodnight Nze.

Goodnight, baby.

"Jasmine, Jas!"

My eyes went to Arinze's mother. She stood before me with her hands on her hip and a frown.

"Are you okay, my dear? I've been calling you, but you seem to be in your own world."

I flinched as the seamstress' pin pricked my skin.

"Ah, sorry madam," she said.

I nodded and returned my gaze to Arinze's mom. "I'm fine, ma'am. Sorry I didn't hear you."

"You're sure?"

I nodded and smiled. I wasn't about to tell her that her son had my mind so warped that I wondered if we were in the twilight zone.

"Okay. I was asking if it was too tight, or you want it a bit loose?"

It was Saturday afternoon and I was in Arinze's parent's house. Yesterday morning, Adaugo came over and asked if I'd be willing to wear the *aso-ebi* of the Kalu family. I'd come to know the significance of being included in this honor of wearing the same African fabric print that everyone in the family would be wearing, so I was stunned. My eyes darted to Arinze, and he'd said he was with whatever I wanted to do. I agreed and less than a full day later, the style I picked was sewn and now I was trying it on for any adjustments needed.

"No, ma'am its fine," I responded with a smile.

Adaugo entered the room, balancing some materials in her hand.

"Ada, you need any help?" I asked.

She finally looked up at me. Her lips turned up in a smile. "The style looks great on you. Before I get sidetracked, what color do you like better?"

I glanced at the green, navy blue, and gold color materials in her hand. "These are for the head wrap, right?"

She nodded. "Yeah. Don't worry, Nze gave strict instructions that yours shouldn't be too tight. Ify will make sure the *gele* woman knows."

I rolled my eyes then chose the navy blue. Adaugo and her mother chuckled before Adaugo left the way she came.

"You'll get used to it. It's how the Kalu men are. Proud and over-protective of their women."

I smiled, but didn't offer a response. Arinze and I had our first argument about his interference on little things just this morning. Every time his mother, sisters, or even grandmother invited me to do anything with them, his first instinct was to shut it down. I'd come to learn that more often than not, "what Nze wanted, Nze got." So, they acquiesced.

I understood he wanted to shield me from things I wasn't used to, but I wondered if he was protecting his family from me. If this was strictly business, I wouldn't mind, but he was constantly saying how he wanted us to explore us outside of this contract. His actions were not those of a man that eventually wanted his family to accept his woman.

I'd misread his signals in Montego Bay. Yeah, he explained about the phone call, but if he was interested, he would have asked me about it then. Was I misreading his signals again? Depriving me of getting to know his family or hanging out with them apart from him wasn't giving me a good feeling. They probably thought I complained to him. At the end of the day, they'd love him regardless, but would dislike me. And for some reason I didn't want to face, that bothered me.

Our argument was the only reason he wasn't here right now, pretending to do something for his parents. He and his cousins went to pick up Adaugo's fiancé from the airport. The traditional ceremony was four days away, but he wanted to be here early. His family would arrive later in the week.

Minutes later, the seamstress was done, and I changed back into my sundress. On my way back to the living room, I took a detour to the kitchen for a bottle of water. When I got back to the living room, Adaugo was there stretched out on the couch with her arm to her forehead.

"Tired, huh?" I sat on the chair next to her.

"Girl, you don't know the half. Everyone is pulling me from all directions. I can't wait for the wedding to be over. I want to get to the marriage," she said.

We both turned to her mother who was coming down the stairs. "You and Daniel have known each other for years, but remember what I told you. Once you get married and start living together, things shift. Not for worse, but there is a shift." She sat opposite us.

"Those butterflies you're feeling don't sustain the marriage. Love in action, commitment, patience, forgiveness, compromise, and most of all God, does. Be yourself, but remember you are part of a unit. Give him a safe space to be vulnerable. Don't turn around and use what he tells you as weapons of warfare against him during arguments. Be aware of how your differences affect the health of your relationship. You're not your husband and he's not you. Most importantly, don't tell your business to outsiders. Preserve your female relationships, but realize that being married shifts the dynamics. Don't allow one *sisi* to tell you what they wouldn't tolerate when they don't even have a man."

Adaugo and I laughed.

"You're laughing. Your father and I have been together for forty-two years now. These are the things my mother taught me. Extend grace, but also know who you are. I like Daniel, but heaven help him if he ever makes the mistake of disrespecting you. You think your brother is bad, remember you have crazy cousins as well."

As she continued to talk, my thoughts traveled to my parents. Before all that mess in the press went down, they were all I aspired to be. The love they shared, I dreamed about. The Kalus were a loving bunch and I was glad they welcomed me. Hearing my name pulled me out of my thoughts.

"Uh, yes ma'am?"

"No…I was telling Ada that although she's marrying Daniel, she's also marrying his family. As her husband, he should know where the boundaries lie, but you can't expect him to abandon them. Especially her mother-in-law. I was giving her an illustration using you and my son. When you get married, I asked if she would like it if he turned his back on me."

I was stuck on the "when you get married" part. Disguising my shock, I nodded and said, "Yeah, I get it."

The three of us continued to talk for a while until the house began to fill up. First Arinze's dad came back. As had become a habit, he asked about my day and if I was enjoying myself. Sometime later, Arinze and his cousins entered with Adaugo's fiancé. As she leaped into his arms, I sneak admired the dark chocolate specimen of a man. Now I understood why she was skipping around here like she was in another universe.

Before we could be introduced properly, Arinze grabbed my hand and amid teasing from his family, dragged me down the long hallway.

"Would you slow down. Did you miss me that much?" I teased.

He pulled me into the study and pinned me against the wall. His expression was serious. Leaning his forehead against mine, he whispered, "I missed you. Did you have fun today?"

"Yeah, I did. We went to the supermarket, had lunch at one very fancy restaurant. Then I got fitted." I raised my hand to his cheek. "You okay? I missed you too."

"I am now. You were mad at me. I felt uneasy."

"I wasn't mad, just frustrated." I giggled. "Your grandmother came by with your real wife…"

He lifted his head. "She what?"

I placed my hand on his chest. "Calm down. Your mom handled it."

"I'll talk to—"

"No, you won't. She is skeptical, which is normal." A beat passed between us. "So, you kissing me or what?"

He growled in my ear. "Kissing. Always kissing." He leaned in to capture my lips, but not before saying. "You're with me tomorrow."

12

JASMINE

$\mathcal{A}$rinze's "you're with me tomorrow" meant a one-hour plane ride to Lagos. With the traditional wedding being so close, I was hesitant to leave. I didn't want it to look like we were abandoning the family. But Arinze was adamant, and it didn't take too much convincing to get with his program. We left Enugu right after breakfast, and arrived in Lagos about an hour ago. Arinze had arranged for early check-in at one of the luxurious hotels in a place known as Victoria Island. We checked in to our premier, adjoining suite on the top floor.

Leaning against the railing on the balcony, I took in the city Arinze referred to as the New York of Nigeria. In the short history lesson that he gave, he described Lagos as a port megacity built on many islands. I peered down, observing the super-fast pace at which everything moved. I thought the horn honking was excessive in Enugu. Lagos drivers were on a whole other level with it.

Before we reached the hotel, Arinze took me to the site of Tune Up that he and his cousins were building here, and it was beautiful. From the little I'd seen, I could describe the city as a chaotic beauty.

I turned around and took some more pictures for the 'Gram with the island as a backdrop. I'd checked in on Aubree and Aunty Delia as I waited for Arinze to conclude a meeting he wasn't able to reschedule. We were supposed to be taking a three-hour drive to the neighboring state to see a popular waterfall.

My gaze remained on the city's skyline, blue skies with white, pillow like clouds floating peacefully along. A knock on the door grabbed my attention. Walking through the sliding doors, I went to open it. Arinze's eyes roamed my body and a grin danced at the corner of his lips. I smoothened down the floral, knee-length, halter dress I had on. I moved back for him to enter.

His hands went to the small of my back. "You look beautiful, baby."

"Thank you. You don't look too bad yourself." I scanned over the simple, seemingly inexpensive black polo shirt he wore over light brown khaki shorts. The Givenchy loafers on his feet, and the Movado on his wrist told a different story. His sunglasses were balanced on his head.

"Thank you, baby. You ready?" He placed a kiss on my forehead.

"Yes, I can't wait."

"Let's be out then. Our private tour guide is scheduled to meet us by noon."

I picked up my backpack that had a change of clothes in case I needed it, my sunglasses, and a bottle of water. Arinze took my hand in his and we headed to the elevators.

"Jas, we're here." I heard Arinze's voice close to my ear. I thought it was a dream until he nipped my earlobe with his teeth.

"Stooopp." I straightened by body which had found its way to his during the journey.

"Quit whining, woman. I was being the perfect tour guide when you fell asleep on me mid-sentence." He shook his head. "I should be the one whining. I was using my Olu Jacob's voice and all."

I laughed at him, looking out of the window to take in our surroundings. "Your what? Who's Olu Jacobs?"

"He's one of Nigeria's legendary actors. There's only one Olu Jacobs, but if I were to draw a comparison, I'd say he's like America's James Earl Jones."

I nodded my head. "Got it. Apologies for letting your talent go to waste."

"You good. When we get to the important talents, I'mma make sure you're alert to enjoy the full experience."

I rolled my eyes at him, ignoring his innuendo. I already had a hard time keeping my thoughts and hormones in check around him. "Are we getting out or do you wanna keep being nasty?"

He chuckled then got out and rounded the car to open the door for me. After giving the driver some instructions, we walked a short distance to meet our guide. They talked fast, in a mix of pidgin and another language. From the hand gestures and the little I could grab, I realized that Arinze had the attraction closed for two hours so we'd have some privacy.

"What language was that? I recognized the pidgin, but the other?" I asked as we walked closer to the waterfall.

"Yoruba."

"You speak your mom's language too?"

Arinze smiled and nodded. "And French and a little Spanish."

"Look at you, all multi-faceted."

He winked. "And multitalented. Don't forget multi-talented."

Shaking my head, I didn't offer a response. Instead I pulled him along. I was excited to see this waterfall he'd been bragging about. We listened as the guide explained how to get to the falls. Hand in hand, we made the short walk through the parking lot until we came upon some winding steps. We followed the guide to the top where there was a rest/refreshment area. Neither Arinze nor I wanted to stop, so we continued.

The views were amazing, so I took out my phone and began taking pictures along the way. The path narrowed across a walkable bridge. The guide pointed out that there used to be a cave there in the days of old. The now collapsed cave used to be a rest stop for farmers. He offered to take us in, but Arinze and I quickly declined. Once we passed the cave, the sound of gushing water became louder. Soon after, we were at the base of the seven ridge fall. It was a sight to behold. Nature at its best, idyllic, serene, and fascinating.

"There are seven different cascades that make up these waterfalls. Founded in 1140, each level has its own flowing fountain. Legend has it that the granddaughter of one of the founding fathers went on a journey of relocation. On the seventeenth day, she settled in this area with her family. One day, some farmers from her household went out into the forest and saw what they called a god, pouring water from a big pot." The guide pointed toward what would be the seventh level of the falls.

He further went on to explain how the people, grateful for the gift of flowing water from the gods, decided to give human sacrifices to show their gratitude. That was the highest gift they could give, in their opinion. After the queen died, the prince, who ruled over the area, decided to take a risk and replace the human sacrifice with animals. He didn't want anyone else to lose their life. Even at the caution of some of his counsel that the decision might stop the water from flowing, he sacrificed animals to spare humans.

Over the course of the next hour, we explored the first fall, then had an almost twenty-minute climb to the second. Arinze offered to carry me to the third level, and I refused. Reaching the third level, I told myself that if I didn't work out for the remainder of this trip, this was enough. Arinze and I allowed ourselves to get a little wet at this level. We played like we were kids. We played rapid-fire twenty questions, splashing water for each time one of us failed to answer within the required time. I hadn't laughed so much in a long time.

At one point, I nearly lost my footing and Arinze grabbed me. Pulling me closer to him, he stared into my eyes. Suddenly, there was a shift in the atmosphere. The water was cool and the breeze was doing its thing, but I felt heat from our connection.

"You good?"

"Yeah…sorry, too much fun. Got carried away."

Arinze pecked my lips. "Don't ever apologize for enjoying yourself. If you let me, I'll always be there to catch you."

I cleared my throat and tried to back away.

He kissed my forehead and chuckled. "Scary."

I didn't even deny it. I was scared. Deliciously so. He flirted a lot, we kissed and felt on each other even more. We stayed a little longer as the guide gave us more history of the people and the evolution of the tourist site. Deciding that the third level was as far as we wanted to go, we started our descent.

After we changed out of our wet clothes, Arinze gave the guide a tip and we made our way back to the car. As we made our way back to Lagos, I showed Arinze the pictures I had taken. I wanted him to help me choose the best picture for Instagram. After initially frustrating my efforts, he finally helped me decide. A few minutes later, a yawn escaped my lips and Arinze pulled me closer to him. I was exhausted, but my spirit was full. Thankful for the wonderful experience and the man I got to share it with.

"Remember, the water has to come to a rolling boil." The cooking class instructor strolled through the length of the kitchen studio.

"I coulda told you that," Arinze whispered in my ear.

I nudged him away from me. This man had a running commentary on everything the instructor said. I'd been the sole recipient of his whispered jokes and cracks since the class started. Then when I laughed, he'd have on a straight face like he wasn't the cause. These people probably thought I was crazy. I cut my eyes towards him, and he winked at me. The instructor was at the other end of the room, so I turned to Arinze with my hand on my hip.

"Would you stop playing around? I almost burned our Jollof rice messing around with you. Don't make me mess up this fufu."

Arinze stood behind me, then wrapped his arms around me. He nuzzled my neck and I leaned into him. "Messing with you is becoming my favorite pastime."

"Wrong time, wrong place."

He took a stance like he was in a stage play. "My desire for you cannot be contained to a specific time or place."

I giggled. "Man, if you don't take your fake Shakespeare—"

"You clowning my skills?"

"These skills, yes."

His rebuttal was cut short when the instructor came to the center of the room and began demonstrating how to pour the yam flour in the water and turn. I didn't have the spatula place-ment right and was getting frustrated when Arinze slipped in behind me and put his hand over mine and guided my movements.

I was trying so hard to concentrate on the food we were making, but got distracted by the way he moved behind my body and his breath grazing my neck as he whispered, "Just like this."

This was our third and final day in Lagos. I was owed noth-ing. That evening after returning from the waterfalls, we were spent. After a shower, we ordered room service and decided to watch a film which ended up watching us. Sometime during the night, I found myself back in my bed.

The next day, we went to the famous Nike Art Gallery. The reason I knew it was popular was because I'd seen it on so many Instagram reels. Arinze got the owner to take us around herself. Being surrounded by so many pieces of art fed the creative in me. After a hearty lunch, we visited some other sites before we retired to rest up for the evening activities. The lounge we went to was for the grown and sexy. With soothing music as a backdrop, I was treated with various finger foods. Meat pies, suya, and goat meat pepper soup. Now that, I did not touch. On the way back, Arinze took the scenic route, showing me the city. Lagos in the night was a sight to behold. Especially the Lekki bridge.

This morning after breakfast, we started on our day. Arinze asked if I wanted to attend a cooking class for fun. According to him, I was killing him slowly when I'd moan when eating local delicacies. And since I'd been saying I loved them so much, he wanted to know if I wanted to learn to cook some of them. I jumped at the opportunity.

When we arrived, I could tell the owner set this up specifically for foreigners and tourists. Everything was so simplified. There were five other couples with us. We made puff-puff first. It was a staple Nigerian snack made of fried dough. Arinze refused to let me help. He took the lead, saying the snack made up his childhood and if I messed it up, he would be traumatized. The second meal was the famous Jollof rice which almost got burned because he chose that time to tell me some joke I didn't even get. Making fufu was the last lesson of the class.

"You see? Teamwork."

Arinze stepped away and the loss of heat from my body made me roll my shoulders. I looked up at him and smiled.

"Thank you."

He kissed my temple. "I always got your back, baby."

Instead of a response, I leaned in and kissed his lips lightly.

This would soon be over, and I'd be back in Atlanta. I loved our evolving friendship. Lately, I'd been contemplating if I'd be able to stick to the rules I set, or if I could take a risk and let the chips fall where they may.

13

ARINZE

"You should be thanking me. In fact, *ehn*, Nze, you owe me for life."

Answer me beautiful. Do I need to come up there?

I lifted my eyes from the text I'd sent Jasmine about ten minutes ago. I turned my gaze to Cheta who was sitting across from me. It was almost eight a.m., and we were having breakfast out on my deck. With Cheta were Jidenna, Qadir, and Qasim—my cousins on my mom's side; Daniel, Adaugo's fiancé, and two of his cousins. I was about to respond to Cheta when Jasmine's text came through. He'd been singing that "you owe me for life" song since Jasmine and I returned from Lagos last night.

Jas Bae: Good morning handsome. My bad. I've never in my life prayed for a full hour straight.

I cackled and sent her a couple of laughing emojis. When we got back last evening, we came straight to my house with plans to just chill. After all the activities we'd embarked on, we needed to be well rested for the wedding. We were interrupted when my cousins, Qadir and Qasim, arrived from Ibadan. I'd completely forgotten they were coming in a day early. Cheta and Jidenna were host to Daniel and his folks while I was away, so they came over as well. Jasmine met everyone and retreated to her room.

The only people that knew about my arrangement with her were Cheta and Jidenna. I didn't even look at that nonsense arrangement as anything that was between us anymore. As far as I was concerned, it was only the conduit that brought us back together. This was my second chance with her, and I wasn't letting her slip through my fingers again. She played the role with me, but when we were around my family, she shrunk. She claimed that she really liked them so lying to them made her feel a way. I told her not to look at it as lying, but her scary behind changed the subject.

I'd felt bad that she was in the room by herself, so I texted my sister, asking her to come over and keep her company. That was my instruction. Keep her company. Next thing I knew Jasmine was packing some of her stuff. Talking about she was sleeping at my parent's house with the women.

I tried to shut it down, because I didn't want her out of my sight while we were here. My grandmother already did too much. I still had to have a conversation with her. My folks were more open minded. Of course, they'd wanted me with a Nigerian, particularly an Igbo lady, but at the end of the day, my happiness trumped their concerns.

Jas Bae: It's not funny. If you had told me I'd be in a prayer meeting last night, I would've stayed.

I remember when we were kids, the whole family gathered in my grandparents' house for morning devotion. It was early since we had to also prepare for school. My grandmother, mother, and aunties took turns casting, binding, and pleading the blood. If my grandmother caught us sleeping, she was going upside our head. Today was my sister's wedding, so I knew they'd go overboard this morning.

I sent her some more emojis then texted her back.

You must think I'm a heathen.

Jas Bae: Whatever. I'm going to take a shower. I'll see you later.

Call me if you need anything.

"Nze, all this smiling you doing…you good, cuz?" Qadir asked. He was a few years older than Qasim, who was my age-mate. They had two younger brothers who'd be arriving later today with their dad, my mom's older brother. My folks owned Kalu International Inc. and we were living nice. But my uncle was super wealthy. I loved going to their house as a kid.

"I'm cool. Don't listen to this one over here." I nodded toward Cheta.

"Bro, you can play it as cool as you want, but I know you. So, I stand on my statement," Cheta said.

Cheta knew me better than anyone, even Jidenna, but I was not about to let him think he had one over on me. My cousin took cocky to a whole new level, and I didn't have time for him to gloat.

"Ain't nothing wrong with admitting you feeling her," Qadir said. He'd been engaged for a while, but we still hadn't heard about a wedding.

"I'm glad you taking a chance again after that nonsense," Jidenna said.

The thought of Chantel gave me a headache. She still sent me random DMs from different numbers. I checked in with Ciara yesterday and she told me about Chantel popping up at my office. She wasn't going to leave me alone until I had a conversation with her. But I wasn't ready to deal with her.

"Look who's talking. You too, need to take ya own advice," I said.

"Difference is I've had love. That stuff with Chantel wasn't love. You were in heavy lust," Jidenna said, making the guys laugh.

He did have a point. More than anything, my ego and pride were bruised by her deception.

"Anyway, if it's real, hold on to it. Be honest with her." Qasim let out a loud sigh.

Everyone turned to him. I furrowed my brows. "Why are you in your feelings?"

"He saw his girl a few months ago. Been plotting. Since then, he goes from anger, to remorse, back to anger," Qadir answered with a smirk.

"You mean the Moroccan chick? I thought things were over between you two?" I asked.

Qasim shook his head. "Nah, I was giving her space, but—"

"No, no, no, that's the wrong move. You don't give the woman you love space." Cheta shook his head. "That only gives her room to listen to unsolicited advice from her friends."

"C, I know you're not talking. You don't even let the women you deal with ride in your car with you," Jidenna said,

"Didn't I just say love?" Cheta's eyes moved to each one of us. "Y'all heard me say love, right?"

"Well, all that is about to be over—" Qasim was cut off by Jidenna's ringing phone.

He excused himself to take the call and we resumed eating and gisting some more. I saw Qadir's eyes move towards Daniel. I knew he was about to start some mess.

"Aye, so you about to take my GoGo?" he asked, referring to Adaugo by her nickname.

Daniel chuckled and thumped his nose. "She's belonged to me for a while. This is a formality."

I nodded, proud of Daniel for not cowering. My cousin always thought someone feared him, so I was glad Daniel matched his energy. They were a family of all boys and were as protective as I was when it came to who my sisters dealt with. I'd known Daniel for a while, and he was good for my sister.

"Okay, talk your stuff then. Just make sure I never see her cry." Qasim added his two cents.

"Aye, I know it's too late to ask this, but how do you know she's the one?" Cheta asked.

"I don't—"

He was cut off by our roars. Cheta and Qasim stood, while I scooted to the edge of my chair. I knew this man just didn't say he wasn't certain my sister was the one. "I like you, Danny, but you gonna have to give us more."

"Nze, you know me. I love your sister. Our love has been tested and ain't nothing truer, but still certainty is not a prerequisite for faith. The faith I have in God for our union; the faith I have in how I love her and how she loves me. Not just words but our actions. I may not be certain, but I hope to God I'm right. I intend to do what I been doing and praying." Daniel finished and leaned back in his seat like he'd just given a lecture.

"Next time lead with that," Cheta said.

Daniel chuckled and stared at his phone. "A'ight guys, I'm out. My family just arrived at the airport. Gotta go get them settled in the hotel and stuff. The next time you see me, I'll be coming to get my wife."

He dapped it up with each one of us and left with his boys. His dad had been present for all the previous steps of the traditional rights, but he'd taken ill three months ago and couldn't travel. To ensure the old man didn't totally miss out, we were headed to Senegal in a few days for the church wedding.

After Daniel left, my cousins and I hung out some more before I told them I needed to go find my woman.

With our fingers intertwined, Jasmine and I watched as my sister danced out of our parents' home with her bridal party. I considered my sisters as my babies. After they had me, my parents struggled for six years before they were blessed with Adaugo, Ifunanya, and Chioma, all two years apart.

The Kalu compound had been transformed to a mini carnival. A live band and traditional dancers entertained guests at intervals. Food and drinks were in surplus. Caterers manned the buffet table while bartenders took care of the bar. A few minutes earlier, Daniel, flanked by his mother and uncles had danced into the compound requesting their bride. After a prayer and a couple of announcements, my mom went into the house to get my sister.

Adaugo danced around then finally came to kneel in front of my dad and his brothers. At the end of the row were my grandparents and aunties. My cousins and I were directly behind them.

"So, what's happening now?" Jasmine whispered in my ear.

"Now they're praying for her. Soon, they'll hand her the local drink called palm wine in a cup and ask her to locate her husband in the crowd."

"Interesting."

"Yeah. Other men are supposed to distract her along the way. The fun of it is that she dodges all the calls from others and keeps looking for Daniel."

"There she goes…" Jasmine said.

I glanced at her and smiled. She really seemed to be enjoying herself. Surprisingly, she'd stuck by my mother most of the day, only coming back to my house when she needed to get dressed. I lifted our hands and placed a kiss on the back of hers. She glanced at me with a smile then resumed observing as my sister finally found Daniel.

Adaugo kneeled before him and presented the wine to him. Daniel took a sip, grabbed my sister's hand, and she stood. Amidst cheers and the drums beating in jubilation, the couple danced to my dad and kneeled before him.

"Does this mean that they're married now?" Jasmine asked.

"Yep. Traditionally, they're now man and wife."

Adaugo and Daniel went into the house to change into

matching attires, and the DJ took over. When the couple reappeared, I stood. Taking Jasmine's hand, I led her to the dance floor where the couple was. I handed over two bundles of money to Jasmine and we sprayed the couple who danced to Timi Dakolo's "Obim."

During the course of the evening, my grandmother came over and danced with me and Jasmine. Earlier we had a private conversation. She asked again whether I was sure that Jasmine was who I wanted. She expressed that her initial concern was that Jasmine would take me from the family since she was American. Although Jasmine and I were nowhere near marriage or a committed relationship, I calmed her down, reassuring her that neither Jasmine, nor any other woman could take me away from my family. The woman I chose to spend my life with and my family would hold different places in my heart. It also didn't hurt that Jasmine blended with my family so well. Now, watching my grandmother teach Jasmine Igbo dance steps warmed my heart.

"Okay mama, *o zu go*," I said, wrapping my arms around Jasmine's waist.

My grandmother laughed. "I was trying to teach my daughter the dance steps, so when it's her turn..."

The look on Jasmine's face was priceless, so I quickly navigated my grandmother away.

"You scared, Jas?" I laughed at her.

Tapping on my chest, she responded. "No comment."

I pulled her close and nuzzled her neck. I'd let her be for now, but before we returned to Atlanta, we were going to have a talk.

Two days later, the whole family arrived in Dakar, Senegal for the third and final part of the wedding. The church ceremony would take place tomorrow evening, followed by a reception at the Radisson Blue where we were lodged.

Currently, Jasmine and I were on a private tour of Maison des Esclaves in Gorée Island. I'd visited the site dubbed "house of slaves" years ago and it was a heavy experience. I didn't want that for Jasmine. However, after learning about the history of Udi Hills and the Erin Ijesha waterfalls, she had Googled this place and wanted to visit since we were here.

I made sure I stayed close to her as we walked through the different sections of the house. Sometimes Jasmine would stand with her arms folded across her chest, at other times she would lean against me for support. We were shown where the children were kept before being shipped to South America, then the section where maidens thought to be virgins were held to entertain men before being sold. There was also a section where they kept those who were underweight and needed to be fattened up.

The part of the house that caused Jasmine to burst out into tears was the room where those who resisted were kept. The space was so tight and small that it was impossible to believe that human beings fit in there. I stopped the guide and pulled Jasmine to the side. She rested her head on my chest and sobbed. When she was done, I lifted her shades to the top of her head, then cupped her face in my hands. I dried her face with my thumbs.

"Baby, you wanna stop?" I asked.

She shook her head. "This is insane to me. You hear about what our ancestors went through, you read some of it, but to know they endured this. How do you treat your fellow human…?"

"Remember, Black people weren't considered humans." I drew her close to me and whispered. "We're almost at the end. There's not much else. Are you sure you don't wanna stop?"

After insisting she was fine, we continued the tour. We went through a couple more rooms, then ended up at the corridors where the enslaved were auctioned off and put on ships. The breeze from the Atlantic Ocean did nothing to curb the stench of what happened in that place. As we looked out into the body of water, I thought about those who decided to jump rather than be enslaved in a foreign land.

The next day, Jasmine leaned into me with her arms around

my neck. Encasing her soft body in my arms, we swayed to "Just The Way You Are by Bruno Mars. She shivered as I sang the lyrics in her ear. My sister's wedding had been a simple and intimate affair. I looked around at the reception hall and noticed people were still enjoying themselves. It was almost midnight and the couple had left for their honeymoon.

Jasmine's gleaming eyes met mine, and I lowered my head to kiss her lips. Yesterday had been a hard day for her. Although we visited some lighter attractions and tasted Senegal's cuisine, there was still the air of heaviness surrounding her. Later in the night, she came to my room and climbed in the bed with me. She didn't speak, so I just held her until she fell asleep. It reminded me of when we were in L.A. In that moment, I knew for certain I wanted something long term with her.

I'd seen her sad, angry, upset, crying, and laughing, and there wasn't any part of me that didn't want to keep experiencing those emotions with her. She was scared, but I had to make her see there was nothing to be afraid of with me.

"Have I told you how beautiful you look?"

"Only like a million times." She giggled then moved her hands to cuff the back of my head.

"This makes a million and one. You look beautiful, baby."

Instead of a verbal response, she leaned in for another kiss. She'd initiated kisses between us before, but this was different. She was conveying the feelings she always seemed to finagle her way out of voicing. My body began reacting to the tongue battle we were engaged in. From experience, I knew that sex complicated things, so I agreed to her no sex rule. Besides, since she was still under contract with Rent A Bae, I wasn't going there.

I broke our contact and grabbed her hand and led her out of the ballroom to the massive pool area. The atmosphere carried a slight chill from the ocean that merged with the infinity pool. I removed my jacket and draped it around Jasmine's shoulders.

Her lavender, backless dress did wonders on her body, but was bound to give her a cold if I kept her out here uncovered.

"I want to see where this goes, Jas. Tell me you want that too?" I pointed between the two of us.

"Arinze, I like you, but—"

"No buts."

"But there is a but. Remember we agreed that this was temporary."

"No. You told me it was, and I asked you not to lie to me."

Her eyes shifted from mine, but I guided her face back to me. "Don't you feel what's happening between us?"

"You feel this way now, but what happens when you stop?"

"What are you talking about? We haven't even started yet and you're dooming us to death?" She didn't speak, so I continued. "We both know that love isn't a feeling that survives without action. I'm not saying we're in love, but don't you want to see where this leads?"

"I was engaged once…"

Those words knocked me back. I knew of the Derrick guy, but I didn't know they were engaged. She must have seen the confusion in my eyes.

"No, not to Derrick. Before him. His name was Edward. We were so in love, until we weren't. I couldn't rise from the depression of my grief when my parents died, and he decided he didn't have it in him to stick around until I did. I've experienced too much loss to want to put myself out there again."

"I'm sorry that happened to you, and I can't promise you I'll be the perfect man. What I can promise you is consistency, stability, protection, and my undying love."

"Arinze—"

"Give us a chance, baby."

She furrowed her brows. "I thought it was women who were affected by wedding blues."

I cackled. "Baby, I don't know about all that. What I do know is this was never a game for me. You were too scary, and I didn't want to fan the flame."

"This is gonna be the last time you call me scary."

"Prove me wrong then?" I challenged.

"I intend to."

I leaned in and planted a kiss on her that sealed our deal.

14

JASMINE

It couldn't be five a.m. already.

Lifting my hand from the snooze button, I rubbed my eyes and detangled my legs from the sheets. It was Wednesday and I desperately wanted to sleep in, but this was Aubree's free day. She was going with me to the wholesale flower market. I had one hour to be ready, so we'd be there when they opened at seven a.m.

After reading the verse of the day on my Bible app and saying a prayer, I made my way to the bathroom. Clean teeth, and a warm shower later, I stood in my walk-in closet trying to decide what to wear. I chose a light sweater to help ward of the chill of the early November morning. Pairing it with my favorite pair of dark denim jeans, I headed to my bedroom swaying to "Gracefully Broken" as Tasha Cobbs Leonard spit words that pierced my soul.

Several minutes later, I was dressed and had my hair in an updo with a bang. I finished off my light face beat with some lip gloss. Picking up the folder with my order invoices, my purse, phone, and keys, I headed to the kitchen to make my smoothie.

If this wasn't intense living, I didn't know what was. In the five months since I'd been back from Africa, it was as though my life was in constant motion. My mom always said to be careful about what you ask for, while Aunty Delia always said be ready for what you pray for. They both had been right. The past few months had seen so many changes that I sometimes lay on my bed after a day of pure exhaustion trying to remember what my life was before now. Mundane was always the word that came to mind, but that existence was now a distant memory.

I was no longer an employee, but a whole business owner out in these streets. Once the money from Rent A Bae hit my account, I went to Ms. Ruby and started the process of buying the shop. Something seemed to have changed with her from the last time we talked, because she ended up selling it to me for thirty thousand dollars less than what she quoted me previously.

Two weeks later, Luxe Petals became a reality. I put in my two weeks' notice and began hiring contractors to make some modifications to the shop. With the extra money, I was able to upgrade the flower cooler and knock down some walls to expand the design area. The shop was now more spacious and airier.

I launched my website and had a soft opening. I started with custom work and in store pickups. Soon after I was able to get a secondhand delivery van and hire an intern. There were days I was certain I'd made a huge mistake. I second guessed myself a lot, but Aubree and Arinze were right there to pull me off the overthinking ledge. Business wasn't booming, but it was good. Better than what I expected. Some of my clients did follow me and Arinze sent some business my way.

Arinze.

We'd been official since that night in Dakar, and I couldn't be happier. Well, that's after I stopped waiting for the other shoe to come flying out to smack me in the face. When we arrived back in Atlanta, he catered to me in ways I didn't know I needed. We had thought-provoking conversations about every topic one could imagine. He challenged and supported my goals and dreams. He prayed with and over me and was consistent in the way he handled me.

I learned pretty quickly that he had a hard time telling me no, but when he did, there was no wiggle room. The way he expressed his feelings for me scared me so much that instead of leaning into it, I started looking for the red flags that would validate my cynicism.

A month after we returned, he left for Australia, headed to the set of the movie he was acting in and consulting on. I missed him like crazy and the time difference was giving us the blues. Going from date nights and chilling with him and his cousins and playing dolls with his niece to having days when I didn't hear his voice at all made for a breeding ground for every negative scenario I could imagine.

I heard a preacher say once that whenever your thoughts are centered on negativity, the devil would help you gather the evidence for validation. That he did. One night, I was so frustrated that I decided to scroll through TikTok. The more I watched videos about horror stories about African men, the more they appeared on my feed. There were beautiful stories from women who called themselves Naija wives, but those did nothing for me. The darkness in my soul enjoyed the horror stories of betrayal, cheating, and desertion.

The next day, I picked a fight with Arinze and then refused to answer his calls. It was so silly and juvenile, but I was on a mission to end what we had going on, before he had the chance to do it first.

I should've known distance wasn't going to stop him. Two days later, Cheta called telling me his cousin says I should get in the car he was sending over. The only thing I needed was my passport and some essentials. I and Cheta had a pretty good relationship, so he gave me a heads up that I didn't want his cousin showing out.

So I did what I was told. A couple of hours later, I was

flying first class to Melbourne. After he scolded me, I made it up to my man all weekend long. We had been okay ever since then.

The doorbell rang, jolting me out of my trance. The girlie was always on time. I looked through the peephole then started to unlock the door when my phone buzzed. I let Aubree in, hugged her and smiled at my caller ID. She shook her head and walked into the house.

"Hey babe, it's 4 a.m. there. Why aren't you sleeping?" I asked Arinze who was in L.A.

"*Obi m*, how are you?"

My lips turned up in a smile at the name he started calling me a few weeks ago. *Obi m* meant "my heart" in his language.

"I'm good, babe. Bree just got here. I'm about to make a smoothie and head out."

"Smoothie is not food." He grunted. "Say hi to Bree for me."

I giggled and walked into the kitchen. "Bree, Nze says wassup?"

She popped her head out from the refrigerator and yelled hi to him.

"A smoothie is gonna have to do. I need to be out the door. But you didn't answer my question."

"Just got back to my condo. I know you have a busy day ahead so I wanted to hear your voice before I lie it down."

"Aww, you're so sweet."

"Aye, cut it out. I'm not sweet," he teased.

"Okay, you're so mannish."

We laughed. I sat on the bar stool while Aubree prepared the fruit and blender for our smoothies. He started to yawn, and I told him to go and lie it down. He was coming back this weekend and I wanted him to get in as much rest as he could before then. We said our goodbyes and I was about to hang up the phone when he called my name.

"Wassup?"

"Don't wanna interrupt your day, but you think you'll be done by say, six?" Arinze asked.

"Probably around eight. Remember I told you I'm having an early dinner with a childhood friend." I felt Aubree's disapproving gaze on me, but I couldn't look at her now. "Why?"

"Nothing. Can't I want to talk to my woman at the end of the day?" he asked.

My stomach sank. But I wasn't doing anything wrong. At least that's what I was telling myself. "You can talk to me anytime. I'll call you when I get in."

He told me he'd be waiting and that he missed me, then we disconnected the call. I turned to Aubree who had her hand on her hip shaking her head.

"Don't start, Bree."

"Nah, sis. I didn't say anything. It's your conscience speaking." She cut up some bananas. "As you requested, that man has tried as much as possible to shield you from the public eye. But you forget this is still his city. He and his cousins are everywhere. Why you're setting yourself up for failure like this is what I'll never understand."

"I'm not doing anything wrong. Derrick is in town and asked to take me to an early dinner."

"It's mighty funny how now that you've moved on from his behind, he finds a way to be in Atlanta every other month." She put all the fruit in the blender. "I be seeing those Nigerian weddings all over the internet. Those folks be turnt and now you're trying to sabotage any chance I have to wear that uniform thing they be wearing."

"Stop being dramatic. Derrick is a friend. He—"

"A friend you used to have sex with. What part of this are you not getting?"

Despite how our relationship turned out, Derrick was there to help me pick up the pieces Edward left behind. He had always been there for me until we added sex to the mix.

Also, I hadn't told Aubree, neither did I ask Arinze about it, but I'd been feeling uneasy lately. I knew I had no business snooping, but the last time Arinze was in Atlanta, he asked me to choose some pictures from his recent studio session and upload to Instagram. We were in his house, and he was cooking us dinner. I did what he asked, but I found myself in his DMs. He hadn't given me any reason not to trust him, so I exited, but not before my eyes caught the handle @iamchantel. I knew she was his ex.

He had read the messages but hadn't responded; however, the messages were recent. He never told her to stop contacting him, so he must be okay with it. That day I was in my feelings and let my insecurities take a hold of me. It happened to also be the day Derrick called to say that he was coming to town and wanted to see me, so I agreed. I knew I wasn't going to do anything with him. But I needed something familiar. Maybe it wasn't such a good idea, but I couldn't tell him no now.

"Bree, I promise, it will be fine. One dinner and that's it," I said. "If for nothing else, closure."

"The disrespect was all the closure you needed. But do you." She shook her head and blended our drinks. While she poured them into our travel mugs, I cleaned up.

"I'll always be there for you, no matter what happens. But if you mess this up, I'm beating you up first, then giving you my shoulder to cry on."

I rolled my eyes, laughed, and threw my arms around her shoulders as we left the house.

Balancing the luxury arrangement in my arms, I closed the door to the cooler room. I picked up the invoice on my design table and walked out to the front of the store. The day had flown by like a blur and this was my last customer before I shut it down.

I lifted my forearm to cover the yawn that escaped my lips. I desperately wanted to lay down in my bed, but I wouldn't be able to do that for another couple of hours. This was what acting off emotions got me. I hadn't anticipated how busy I'd be, and I still had to meet Derrick in an hour.

"Here you go, Mr. Kenton."

I set the lavish, lavender bouquet down on the counter. My very distressed customer disconnected his phone call and walked toward me.

He rubbed the back of his neck, glancing at the arrangement, then his eyes met mine. "Thank you. You're sure this will do the trick?"

How you forget your wife's birthday was a mystery to me, but I designed the heck out of this bouquet to appease her. Looking at the stargazer lilies, lavender roses, and purple carnations I'd put together for his emergency request, I reached for the care instructions.

"I'm not a miracle worker, but you said her favorite color is purple. Add this with some jewelry, and you probably won't have a long groveling period."

He thanked me again, picked up the vase and left the shop. He'd called earlier frantic. My heart ached for him, so I squeezed him in, but made sure to collect payment up front. I walked to the door, turned over the open sign and locked it. I walked to the back room which I carved out for my office to pack up my things. Turning off the lights, I headed out using the back entrance. Opening my car, I put my stuff in the passenger seat. My phone buzzed with a text.

Derrick: On my way, can't wait to see you Jas.

Before I could dwell on the queasiness in my stomach, another text came through.

Bae: Headed to W. Hollywood. Don't stay at the shop too late. Call u later.

Ok, baby. I texted back.

I rubbed my chest to ease the ache Arinze's text brought on.

"Girl, I'd have chest pain too if I had to deal with your man's cousin."

I heard the voice behind me and laughed out loud. It was my neighbor, Reign. I turned to her. She was leaving her shop as well. She owned a skin care store about three doors down from me. The first day I talked to her, she seemed standoffish, but I had gotten to know her a little better in the past couple of months. We weren't exactly friends, but we'd had lunch together a few times.

"Hey, girl. Nah, I'm good and Cheta is not that bad."

She waved me off. "The fact you had to put 'that' in front of bad should tell you something."

I laughed at her again. Whenever Arinze was away working and Cheta was in Atlanta, he'd pop up at the shop to check on me. One of such times, he met Reign. Let's just say they couldn't stand each other, but Cheta made it his mission to pick on her regardless. Reign and I talked for a little bit before we said our goodbyes. All in all, it had been a good day.

I got almost everything I needed from the wholesale market earlier. Aubree had helped me offload the flowers and sort them for temporary storage. We then ordered something to eat while I assembled the orders for delivery. After eating, Aubree had to leave. That was about the time my intern came in.

Tyler was in high school and worked only a couple of hours after school each day. While she manned the front, I designed some last-minute delivery requests, including Mr. Kenton's. I couldn't afford to hire anyone, but Arinze refused to let me drive around Atlanta delivering flowers. So, he insisted on hiring a part-time driver for me to make deliveries on the days I had them.

Arinze was already upset that I refused any other assistance he offered, so I let him have this. I wasn't one of those girls that subscribed to the "I don't want him for his money mantra." If it was something else and he offered, I wasn't going to say no. He was my man.

But this, Luxe Petals, was different. From watching the older Kalu men and their wives, I understood that culturally, Arinze was wired to take over and "make things better," but I didn't want that for this shop. Luxe Petals was more than a shop; it was a journey to self-actualization. Victory after all the things I put off, being afraid and depressed.

The next thing I had to do was close this open-ended chapter with Derrick for good. I broke things off with him before I left for Nigeria, but I was also aware that both of us fed on this toxic cycle of resurrecting what was dead. Each for our own personal reasons.

An hour later, seated across from Derrick at Mary Mac's in the heart of Ponce de Leon, I embraced the love/hate relationship I had with myself over the decision to be here. On the one hand, the food was the bomb. Like out of this world good for the soul. I'd think about the calories later, but this fried cube steak with brown onion gravy was touching the spot. But Derrick trying to convince me that I was better off sticking to what I knew—him— was seriously irritating me.

Derrick leaned forward to buttress the point he'd been making for the last twenty minutes. "Jas, I get the whole pretend thing. I couldn't be prouder of what you've done with the shop, but I ain't know you were gonna do it for real."

Leaning back in my chair, I crossed my arms over my chest. "D, we didn't work. If I had known this was what you wanted to talk about, I wouldn't have come."

"Don't be like that. I wasn't settled, and you were out there making moves. I didn't have the time to focus on us. But look..." He pointed at the offer letter he'd shown me earlier. "I got the job I been wanting with Coca Cola. I'm ready to do this right."

Staring into his eyes, I knew for certain that what I had with Arinze was real. Not only was my man the busiest person I had ever dated – an actor, businessman, spokesperson for some brands while keeping his close-knit family together - but he always made me a priority. I never felt like an afterthought.

But here I was… trying…heck I didn't even know what I was trying to do. But meeting Derrick was a mistake. I moved my empty plate to the side and placed my hands on the table.

"D, we were good friends before we complicated it with sex. But what we had was never love. I'm to blame as well. I held on to you not because I was in love with you, but because I was afraid to lose the familiar."

"Jas, I refuse to believe we didn't have something special. We've known each other for…" Derrick placed his hands over mine and slowly massaged the back of my hand with his thumb in a circular motion.

He always did this when he wanted me to acquiesce to his way of thinking. I was about to withdraw my hand from his touch when I felt an overwhelming presence approach the table. I turned and met Cheta's menacing eyes. He signaled to the men he was with to proceed to their table. As he moved closer, I removed my hands from the table. That probably made me look guiltier, but from the look he was giving me, he'd already drawn his conclusions.

"Jazzy Jas, what's up?" Cheta was addressing me, but kept his eyes on Derrick.

Derrick shifted under Cheta's gaze, but remained silent.

"Hey C, I didn't know you were in town," I stuttered.

Ignoring me, he sized up Derrick. "Introduce me to your friend."

"Erm… Cheta this is Derrick, a friend of mine. Derrick this is—"

"I know who he is…"

The bass in Derrick's voice had me shifting in my chair. Cheta on the other hand, thumbed the tip of his nose, smirked, and turned to me for the first time.

"Let me rap with you real quick." Cheta assisted me up and I followed him to the corner.

"Look, Che—"

"I like you, Jas. You're good for my cousin. I haven't seen Nze happier, but I won't allow another woman to take him down a path—"

Heat shot up through my body at his nerve. "I don't know what you thought you saw but I—"

Cheta put his hand on my shoulder to stop my rant. He bent a little to meet my eyes. "I saw a man who wants you and a woman with compassion in her eyes." He patted my shoulder and walked off.

I wanted to cuss him out, but nothing about what he said was wrong. Therefore, I was madder at myself. The Kalu cousins were close. I didn't want to find out how close, so I was going to come clean with Arinze before Cheta had a chance to.

15

ARINZE

"**C**raziest thing I've ever done…let me think."

Jasmine placed her index finger under her chin and tilted her head. I nuzzled her neck, soliciting a giggle. The floral, citrus scent she had on drove me crazy. That and everything else about her.

"Nze, leave the girl alone so she can tell us the story," DJ said.

Tonight, we were having dinner in my friend, DJ and his wife's cabin in Big Sur. I missed my woman, and nobody was going to keep me from being all over her. For the past few weeks, between being on set and making sure everything was on the up and up for the premier of *Blurred Vision*, I'd been in an out of Atlanta a lot. Although Jasmine and I talked about twice every day, I needed her presence.

I'd asked her more than once to fly out to where I was to spend the weekend with me, but I understood that her flower shop was new, and she didn't want to leave it unattended. Two days ago, I flew into Atlanta, handled some business, picked up my woman and headed right back to Big Sur. This was the calm before the storm. After the premiere tomorrow night, I could breathe easier.

"You don't mind, baby. Do you?" I asked.

Jasmine pecked my lips. "Of course not."

Dinner was over and we were in the kitchen. DJ was putting away the last of the clean dishes while Chloe, his new wife, leaned against the opposite side of the island where I had Jasmine encased.

"You guys are so cute," Chloe said.

"Y'all please don't get her started. My wife thinks she's everybody's cupid," DJ fussed, wiping his hand with a dish towel.

Chloe walked to her husband and kissed his lips. DJ leaned against the sink and drew his wife to him. Her back rested flush with his chest. "But I was somehow responsible for this match." She pointed between Jasmine and me. "They met at my wedding."

I wrapped my arms around Jasmine's waist. Slipping my hands under the green camisole she wore over distressed black skinny jeans, I rubbed her stomach. One thing I quickly realized was I had to have my hand on some part of her body when she was in my presence.

Jasmine resumed her story. "Okay, check this. When I was sixteen, my dad had just directed a movie that was a huge success at the box office. All of a sudden, everyone wanted to know about the Bowmans."

My hands stopped moving, trying to gauge if there was an inflection in her voice. Over the past couple of months, she talked about her parents more. There was less pain than when she first told me about them. I squeezed her waist giving her the strength she needed to continue.

"Paparazzi were now interested in their only daughter and decided to start hanging out in my school where I hung out with friends. So, I decided to wear the same outfit every day and did the exact same thing for a month. They had nothing to write about." Jasmine shrugged.

Everyone laughed and I shook my head and pulled her even closer to me. The first day she told me that story, I had insight into how petty she could be when she felt backed into a corner. We continued sharing stories of crazy things we'd done when my phone buzzed.

Cheta: Change of plans cuz. Can't make it to LA tonight but I'll be there in the AM

I responded *No wahala* and placed the phone back in my pocket. NBA season had begun, so I knew that Cheta was cutting it close. I told him not to stress himself, but one thing about my family, we would move mountains to be there for one another. My sister and her husband, along with Jidenna and my niece were arriving in the morning. Cheta was the only one meant to be here later tonight.

It was a big night for me and these past two days of winding down with Jasmine was just what I needed. We'd been by to see her aunt and uncle and spent time with them.

I couldn't believe this woman had me interested in horses. She nearly flew out of her skin when I surprised her with tickets to the Travers Stakes race horsing event in Saratoga. We stayed in an inn, enjoying the festivities of the weekend. After getting her back on a plane to Atlanta, I flew across the country for work. The other day, I teased her about not placing her horses above our children. She laughed, but I was dead serious.

Jasmine coming into my life provided the perfect balance I needed. She was my calm for the storms I faced outside. She wasn't someone who thought she and I were in competition for anything. She was kind, strong willed, but willing to learn as was I. She taught me patience. Her heart was delicate and even though it was in my nature to be more aggressive, I had to tone it down for her. I needed to ground her in the safety that I could provide her. I couldn't imagine the losses she'd endured, but I knew how they scarred her. My job was to make sure it didn't hurt as bad as it used to.

I was serious about us building a family together. I knew it hadn't even been a year yet, but when a man knows, he knows. I'd talked to my folks since we've been back from Enugu. They all took a liking to Jasmine. The key thing my parents hammered on was to be sure she was the one before I made any promises. She was, but as often, she had this wall up. No matter how much I showed her I'd be there, I could feel her trying to protect herself, just in case.

For the past two days, we'd done a little of everything. The five-bedroom cabin was located along the towering cliff of Big Sur. The suite Jasmine and I occupied had unobstructed, panoramic views of the Pacific Ocean which we took advantage of while having private meals. When we weren't indoors, we went for wine tastings, hot air balloon rides and long walks by the beach.

"A'ight y'all, movie time," Chloe announced.

I grabbed one bowl of popcorn while DJ grabbed the other. The ladies carried the drinks, and we made our way to the outdoor theatre. There was a fire going in the marble fire pit while the area was surrounded by tiki lamps. We placed the snacks on the table in the center of two sofa beds. I pulled Jasmine down on my lap, and she got comfortable between my legs. I drew her closer to my chest while I leaned against the backrest. She threw a light blanket over us.

"I hope you're having a nice time," I whispered in her ear.

She tilted her head so her eyes could meet mine. "The best. Thank you." She turned her head back to the screen, then faced me again. "Who was that earlier? Everything all right?"

"Yeah, it was Cheta." I felt her body stiffen. I frowned and peered down at her. "You good?" Jasmine and Cheta had a really good relationship last time I checked. They sometimes ganged up against me in a heated discussion, so I wondered what that was about.

"Yeah...yeah...I'm fine."

"He'll be here in the morning instead." I felt uneasy with her reaction and wanted to pry more. If anyone made her uncomfortable, I wanted to know about it. My cousins loved her, but if something had happened, I needed to know. Cheta and I were to meet for brunch tomorrow. I made a mental note to ask him what the deal was.

"Okay, *Pretty Woman* is about to start. Babe, I better not see you cry either. You got us watching this corny movie," DJ joked, and occupied the other sofa with his wife.

"It's a classic," Jasmine chimed in.

"See, Jas knows what's up," Chloe said.

We settled down to watch the movie. After this, we would make the ninety-minute flight back to my condo in L.A in preparation for the whirlwind of the next several weeks.

The day had finally arrived. I woke up to congratulatory messages and prayers from my parents, grandparents, and other members of my family. Dressed in Zeidu joggers with a *Blurred Vision* hoodie, I hung my suit bag across my shoulders and went in search of Jasmine. It was still very early, so I expected her to still be asleep. I, on the other hand had some last minute press to attend to before the night's festivities. My condo was a good distance from tonight's venue, so I wouldn't have time to return home to get ready.

I walked toward my guest bedroom and tapped on the door lightly and waited. With no response, I turned the knob. A grin crept up my lips, observing Jasmine sprawled out on the bed. She was on her stomach with her face towards the door. I leaned over her and peppered kisses on her face and neck causing her to stir.

Peeling her eyes open, she smiled at me. My lips were met with her hand when I lowered my head to kiss her.

"Good morning, Beautiful. I can't kiss you, now?"

With her mouth still covered, she giggled. "Good morning. Not with morning breath."

She tried to scoot off the bed, but I held her down. I tickled her. Laughing and in her bid to get away from me, she removed her hand from her mouth. Using the opportunity, I pecked her lips.

"Don't deny me, woman."

She frowned and I kissed her forehead. "I got to head out now. I have some press and last minute things I need to take care of. You, just chill out and relax until Trent comes to pick you up. Breakfast will be delivered from that spot you like in about an hour. Also, Ciara will be by with some people to get you all dolled up for tonight."

"In all this, you still had time to think about me?"

"Haven't I shown you that you'll always be my number one priority?"

She nodded.

"Words."

She sat up and leaned against the headboard. "Yes, you have."

"Good, so allow me to do me."

After pecking her a few more times, we prayed together, and I left.

Later that evening, I walked to the stage with the cast of the movie to a standing ovation. Looking out into the crowd and seeing the head nods and smiles made the hard work worth it. Earlier when I left my condo, I had expectations. I know the God I serve, but once again I put Him in a box and He exceeded my expectations more than I could imagine. *Blurred Vision* was a hit.

The audience, which consisted of some members of the press, my peers, various media houses, radio, the winners from all over the country who participated in the promotional campaign give-aways and studio executives, all loved it. When the applause died down, I and the executive from the studio I partnered with, gave a message of gratitude. After fielding some questions from the audience, the theatre was cleared out and we all headed to the general area for refreshments.

I kept my eye on Jasmine all night as I mingled with guests. She looked stunning in the cobalt mermaid dress she had on. The sequined material with a high slit fit her perfectly and complimented the glow in her skin. I proudly walked with her on the red carpet, and she carried herself with grace and style. She owned her position in my life. Despite the pride that welled up in my chest as I introduced her to my world, the woman I had come to love was also responsible for the aching disappointment that lay in the pit of my stomach. The one thing I asked her not to do was to lie to me. And despite how patient, reassuring, loving and protective I'd been, she still found the need to.

After meeting up with Cheta, I found myself coming at him for whatever he did to make Jasmine uncomfortable. Her body language when I mentioned his name the day before bothered me. Imagine my surprise when he laughed in my face and told me of her little rendezvous. I'd already dealt with one deceptive woman; I was not willing to deal with another.

As I made my way across the room, I was intercepted by a reporter from Mosaic Magazine. The Nigerian publication was kind enough to send a representative over to cover the event. Answering a few questions, I continued my journey when I heard a voice that caused me to freeze.

"Arinze. Arinze?"

I turned and as I suspected, the tall, lithe figure that was once the cause of my joy and greatest regret swayed toward me. As devious as ever, Chantel knew I couldn't ignore her here. When we were together, I'd talked about fulfilling this dream of mine, so she knew how important today was. There was no need wondering how she got in because she could charm anyone into doing her bidding with ease. I had two options—continue walking and draw attention to my past life, or talk to her in private.

Before I could make my decision, Sean appeared from somewhere and stepped in front of me. He wasn't with me when the thing with Chantel happened, but before he became my body-guard, he intimated himself with the details.

Her forehead creased at Sean. She looked at me. "Really? I just want to talk."

"Ms. Morris…"

I glanced at her with a blank stare before my eyes traveled the room looking for Jasmine. The last time I checked, she was some-where with my sister. Locating them preoccupied in chatter, I returned my focus to Chantel. I patted Sean on his shoulder, and he moved to the side.

"And you thought it best to come here?" I scoffed.

"I've tried to talk or reach you for close to a year. You wouldn't talk to me."

"And that didn't send a message?"

"Please, for old times' sake. You owe me an audience."

My jaw clenched and fists balled at her insinuation. "I owe you nothing. You coming here tells me you'll still do anything to get what you want, no matter who gets hurt." I turned, looking for the next exit. Locating it a few inches away, I turned to her. "Follow me."

"Nze?"

"I got it, Sean. I'll be right back." I reassured him and moved to the door with Chantel hot on my trail.

Finding a free room, I pulled her in.

"Talk. You have two minutes. I need to get back to my date."

She let out a deep breath. "She's beautiful."

I ignored her remark and looked at my watch. There'd never come a day when I'd discuss Jasmine with her.

"What do you want?"

"I want to clear the air. I miss you."

"Are you for real? After five years? What happened to your husband?"

Silence ensued for a few minutes. She stared at me. "We're divorced."

"I can pretend to empathize, but that still doesn't explain why you're here."

"I never meant to hurt you."

"You almost ruined me."

"I know and I regret that but—"

Chiding myself for entertaining the conversation this long, I shook my head and moved toward the door. She moved in front of me. Frowning down at her, I sidestepped her. "I don't have time for your games, Chantel."

I almost got to the door when the next words came out of her mouth. "We were good together. Please give us a second chance."

I cocked my head and dipped my brows at her audacity. "Hear me and hear me good; there'll never be an 'us' again. Besides I can't give you what already belongs to another." Leaving the room, I tossed over my shoulder, "Be warned, Chantel. Stay away."

16

JASMINE

My leg shook with agitation as I glanced at the phone in my hand. Trying hard but failing to ignore the man next to me. His intense stare sent chills down my spine which didn't make sense to me because he hadn't answered my questions, neither had he said anything to me since we'd been at the back of his truck.

We'd had a wonderful time. On so many nights, Arinze and I had discussed *Blurred Vision,* but to see it up on the big screen was nothing short of amazing. I grew up in Hollywood, but mostly behind the scenes. To see the glitz and glamour up front was a different story. I didn't feel out of place because Arinze had made sure I was dressed like a princess.

After he left in the morning, I slept a little longer until the doorbell rang with my breakfast. From then, it was a whirlwind of people coming in and out of his condo all for me. His assistant arrived with the masseuse for my full body massage and facial. Next, I got to meet the designer behind the Zeidu fashions he wears. According to her, the instructions Arinze's gave her were to, "make sure nobody mistakes whose woman she is." From hair to make up to getting to the venue, meeting with the Kalu family then walking the red carpet, everything looked perfect, but I knew my man. Something was off.

From the moment I got to the venue, he was moody and standoffish. I asked a million times if everything was okay. He'd give me a smile I know didn't meet his eyes and redirect the conversation. I chucked it up to stress, not wanting to add more to his plate than necessary. This was his day, and I was there to support him. The way he'd done for me since we met.

Looking at my phone and the picture of him and his ex, entering a room at the same event we just left boiled my blood. I'd been seen with Arinze around town, although the paparazzi had pretty much left me alone, there were some pictures and silly headlines from time to time. When my phone started going off with Instagram notifications, I was alarmed. Then I got a text from Bree.

There must be an explanation. Ask first.

I knew it couldn't be good. The way he had his hand at the small of her back as he escorted her to the room did something to my heart. The caption from a few celeb gossip pages had variations of the same caption.

Chantel and Arinze: Will they get it right this time?

The comments section was a mixed bag. Some people were against the reunion. Some of the comments inquired how I felt about the union. Some even commended Arinze for having his ex and present at the same place and nothing popping off. In that moment, as I struggled for breath, I knew that I loved him. I knew that if we didn't make it, I'd be devastated. It took everything in me to calm down enough not to question him at the event. The last time he got into it at a premiere because of his relationship, it didn't end well. No matter how mad I was, I didn't want to do that.

"Arinze."

"I said not here, Jasmine."

My eyes met Sean's in the rearview mirror. His expression as always was blank. I folded my hands across my chest and turned my back to Arinze. My thoughts were in a frenzy, replaying every moment that led me here. With Derrick, disappointment I was used to. Hurt was a new territory and I hated it.

Once we made it to the condo, I scurried to the elevator. Rage coursed through my veins at Arinze's dismissiveness. Without waiting for him to get on, I rode it up to the top floor where his condo was. Using the key, he'd provided me earlier, I let myself into the condo. The door hadn't closed fully when I heard him barge in. I turned on my heels to face him. His eyes didn't hold the warmth they normally did. They were dark, but I didn't care. He owed me an explanation.

"Arinze, we're not done talking about this," I said to his back as he headed to the kitchen.

"Talk? I thought you wanted to yell baseless accusations at me," he said, without looking at me.

"What was I supposed to do? I'm tagged on numerous pictures and presented with video evidence of you and your ex, and you don't think I should be upset?"

"You have that right. But I expect you to know me well enough to know that there's something not right with the story."

"You expect me to believe that you didn't know she was coming? How did she get into an exclusive event?"

"Yes, I expect you to believe it because I said it. I'm not the one amongst us who has a hard time telling the truth."

I furrowed my eyebrows and placed my hands on my hips. We were now on opposite sides of his island. "What's that supposed to mean?"

"It means that I won't deal with a woman that lies to me. Not ever again."

So, this was the reason for his attitude all evening. Cheta must've gotten to him. I scoffed. "I see Cheta ran his mouth."

"You forget I know you, Jas." He advanced toward me. "The way your body froze when I mentioned Cheta yesterday had me worried." He thumped his head. "Silly me, I thought he did something to you, since I know how he can get. I came at him hard, only for him to tell me you might be jittery because he saw you out with Derrick. The night you told me you were out with a friend!"

"Derrick is a friend!"

"Says the woman who's up in arms about an ex. One I've explained I had to talk to for one minute because I didn't want her causing a scene." He banged the bottle of water down on the island, spilling a little of it.

A few beats passed between us, before he shook his head at me and headed out of the kitchen. I was at a loss because he did have a point. However, there were still some unanswered questions and the fact that the public was placing me in this weird love triangle because of it.

I walked into the living room, but he wasn't there. Following the sound of slamming drawers, I moved toward his room. When I got there, the door was opened so I entered. For a minute, I forgot we were in battle with his well chiseled, bare chest staring me in the face. The way his suit pants hung low on his waist with the belt undone had me salivating.

"Is there something you want, Jasmine?"

The iciness of his tone dowsed me with the cold water I needed to get myself together. I lowered my eyes momentarily before looking in his.

"The dinner with Derrick was harmless. I needed closure," I said.

He leaned against his dresser and folded his arms across his chest. "After almost eight months? Closure from what exactly? From what you told me, he treated you like trash. I–"

"Okay! I was insecure, okay? It was a lapse in judgment."

"Insecure about what? Have I given you any reason to doubt me? I understand hiccups in relationships, so I've been patient. I've been anything you've needed me to be. Your friend, supporter, protector, your safe space. I love you, for goodness' sake, so again, what did you have to be insecure about?"

My lips quavered. I couldn't enjoy his admission of love because my heart thudded against my chest in fear that I'd messed this up.

"I saw her DMs…"

"What are you talking about?"

I went on and explained how I saw Chantel's messages to him and how I ended up with Derrick at dinner. In his eyes was disappointment. The fact that I'd let him down caused shame to rise within me. He was right. He'd been everything I needed when I needed it. Fear caused my lapse. Arinze walked towards me, stopping just before he got to me. I longed for him to pull me to him and reassure me like he always did.

He didn't.

"I'm not mad you went to dinner with Derrick. There's not a man alive that can take what's mine from me unless I freely give it. I don't like it, but that's not the issue. I'm furious that you lied to me. The one thing I asked you not to do. You know why lying is a deal breaker for me. Jasmine, I'm too old to play games. From day one, I've told you my intentions and have been consistent with my energy. If I have to worry about how committed you are to us, then we need to reevaluate.

"I'm exhausted, going to take a shower and then bed. Tonight, was the best night of my life. All I wanted to do was end it with you. But I think you need time to see if this is what you want."

Arinze left me standing there and walked into the bathroom. I'd never felt so low.

I could put together any type of bouquet with little or no brain power. And that was exactly what I'd been doing in the three weeks since I'd been back in Atlanta. The shop was great, my aunt and uncle were healthy, Ella was even her usual self again, but I was miserable. I pressed play on my phone to listen to Arinze's voicemail again. The one that contained all the love he had for me in his voice. I desperately needed that memory to cancel out the last time he spoke to me.

There was a quick knock on my office door before it opened. I stared at my best friend as she rolled her eyes at me and pranced toward my desk.

"It's Friday. Don't you have class?" I asked, watching her slam an envelope on my desk.

"I got someone to cover me, and I'm going to cover you while you go and get your man." She sat on my desk.

I picked up the envelope and opened it. It was a ticket to New York City. That was where Arinze currently was. *Blurred Vision* opened for the public a week after the premiere to rave reviews and impressive numbers. So much so that they had now added it to show in more cities. New York being one of them.

"I don't understand." I looked up at her.

"Listen, you've cried, and you've been moody and I'm tired of it. No one told you to take your behind and run from that man in the middle of the night."

After I left Arinze's room that night, I'd called an Uber to take me to my aunt's house. I left him a note, but I couldn't face him.

"You didn't see how he looked at me. The shame I felt; I couldn't face him…not that he's even reached out to me."

"Heffa, you were wrong! That man has you spoiled so much that you don't know how to act. Look, here's a ticket, your flight leaves in two hours. I've packed your stuff and will lock up the shop. Now go and tell that man you ain't gonna lie no mo'."

I sat stunned before tears ran down my cheek. I'd missed him so much, but the courage to face him eluded me.

"Just go, Jas. Go! He loves you, but I agree, the ball is in your court." Aubree started gathering my things.

Five hours later, I was in Arinze's hotel room at the Renaissance in Manhattan. After the initial shock of Aubree's surprise, I jumped into action. On my way to the airport, I contacted Ciara. After the promise of her favorite chocolates, she gave me the information I needed. Now I was sitting here waiting on Arinze to return.

This was the first night the film was playing in New York, and I wanted to pamper him for a change. I felt I had ruined the night in L.A. From my information, Arinze should be walking into his suite in a few minutes. Since he was on the go so much, he wasn't really eating heavy starches, so I had dijon thyme roasted salmon in the warming oven. But first, he'd enjoy a soak in the eucalyptus and lavender infused bath that I had drawn him. His favorite wine was also on deck. Before I left Atlanta, I placed an order for a gift basket. Two red blends and a golden chardonnay were paired with different kinds of gourmet sweets and savory snacks to which I added two dozen preserved blue velvet roses.

Clicking locks sent my heart into a frenzy. I smelled his signature cologne before I saw him. Walking closer, I came face to face with the man my soul desired. The timber of his raspy voice caused goose pimples to ravish my skin. As I moved closer to his voice, our eyes met, and his shock was palpable.

"Cheta, lemme call you back."

I wasn't sure if he waited for a response because he disconnected the call immediately.

"What are you doing here?" he asked.

Maintaining eye contact, I cleared my throat. "I came to apologize. I want this. I want us. I love you with everything in me." I rattled, afraid to stop for fear of rejection. "Arinze, you came in and healed what was broken in me. The thought of another day without you, guts me. I'm sorry for doubting you."

A few beats passed between us before he moved closer to me. His eyes pinned me in place, but he remained silent. I shifted my weight from one foot to the other, my nerves getting the best of me.

"Please say something," I whispered.

He lifted his hand and cuffed the side of my neck. His thumb gently caressed my cheek. "I pride myself on protecting and being a safe space for those I love. You… are at the top of that list. When you doubt that, my world is off kilter."

"I'm sorry."

"Your apology is fine, but I need your word. Promise to have faith in me. Promise to be completely open and communicate whatever may bother you about us."

Tears dangled on the brim of my eyelids. "I promise; you have my word."

"Good." He thumbed away my tear and pulled me into him for a hug.

I'd missed the comfort of his arms. Wrapping my arms around his waist, I snuggled into him.

Lifting his head from the crook of my neck, he stared into my eyes. "You still gotta make it up to me."

I smiled. "I intend to do that and more."

"Give me those lips."

"With pleasure."

I puckered up and joined Arinze in sealing our reunion with the kind of soul snatching kiss that started it all.

The End

EPILOGUE

Jasmine

The Following Year...

"So, what they about to do now?"

I moved my eyes from the track and cut them at Aubree, annoyed at her frequent interruptions. Although I hadn't seen my friend in a week, now wasn't the time for me to give her a lesson on the Derby. For my birthday, my man made my childhood dream come true.

Watching the Kentucky Derby live.

It was Saturday, the final day of the races and earlier this morning, Aubree, Rich, and Cheta arrived in Louisville to meet up with us. Arinze and I had arrived on Thursday night and the weekend had been nothing short of spectacular. Filled with luxury, a healthy dose of various beverages, lilies, roses, and loads of heart-pumping excitement.

On Friday, we enjoyed a culinary event where master chefs from across the nation made and showcased their mouthwatering dishes and desserts. I had enough macaroons to last me a lifetime. I participated in a race for Breast Cancer and took a VIP, all access backstage tour of the behind-the-scenes action. What made this experience so fulfilling was that Arinze participated in all these activities with me. He still couldn't completely wrap his head around my devotion to the thoroughbreds but cheered on all my excitement.

That was the story of our relationship. Which was stronger than ever. We had our share of disagreements and arguments like any couple. We also had times where our cultures clashed. However, the key to our stability was what he hammered on in the beginning of our relationship. We dealt with each other based on each other. No outside stories or influences.

With his celebrity did come press, good and bad. He always said that if it didn't come from him, it wasn't true. Arinze had been so consistent in his unwavering faith and love for me, that sometimes I felt I wasn't doing enough for him. That idea he quickly dismissed, and if there was one thing I'd learned, it was to be rooted in what we had.

With his status also came an increase in celebrity flower orders. Luxe Petals was no longer the struggling flower shop that made me question my sanity, but it was now thriving. So much so that I was able to hire another full-time designer and venture off into designer balloon event set ups.

"You got one more time Bree or I'm gonna have you sit over there." I pointed to the seats at the other end of our boxed seating area.

I returned my focus to the dirt and turf racetracks for the eleventh race of the day. I giggled when I heard her suck her teeth and mumble something about me being mean for no reason. She stood, and I assumed she walked over to the guys. Rich, Arinze, and Cheta stood in the corner sipping on drinks while I refocused on the track action. The prelude to the main event was starting soon and nothing was about to make me miss the most exciting two minutes in sports. I'd deal with Aubree later. What was about to happen in the next thirty minutes was what the whole weekend was about.

I stood and applauded with the rest of the crowd as the horses approached the finish line. My excited movements stilled when I felt Arinze arms wrap around my waist, his hand moving slowly up and down my silk lilac ZF jumpsuit. I leaned my head back against his chest, careful not to get the feathers of my Ankara rimmed fascinator in his eyes. I inclined my head and got lost in his eyes. I'd been on the other end of them—cold, fiery, distant—but my favorite temperature was their warmth. I'd get lost in them in a heartbeat.

"Did I tell you how much I love you?" I asked.

"Since Thursday? I've lost count." He smiled.

"I'm serious, baby."

"Shoot, I am too. Normally, you ration those suckers out. This weekend, I'm about to overdose." He chuckled.

"We're in public. Can't you people hold on till you get to your room?" Cheta said, taking a seat beside us.

"CK, I never knew you to be a hater," I teased. Arinze was my man, but this guy was like the big brother I'd always longed to have.

"And I ain't. But you two get on my nerves sometimes." He took a picture with the track as his backdrop.

Aubree sat on Rich's lap. "A minute ago, I was getting on her nerves, but Arinze gets a pass. I see you, Jazzy."

I giggled, but before I could speak, Arinze did. "Y'all get off my baby. Her birthday is tomorrow so this weekend is all about her." He peppered kisses along my neck while our friends and family mumbled under their breath.

Arinze sat and pulled me onto his lap. With his arms securing me in place, I kissed all over his face. His smile was something I always wanted to see. He was about to speak when the noise from the stadium grew. I turned back to the tracks and watched as the contenders and their connections walked from their barn in preparation for the race.

I squealed. "Baby, this is it. The main event."

"It's your world, baby. Enjoy."

Soon after, the jockeys were told to mount, and the marching band began to play, "My Old Kentucky Home." I stood and moved closer to the rail of our boxed seats. I'd sung this song so many times from my living room watching the Derby on NBC. Here now with thousands of fans, my adrenaline couldn't be contained.

I glanced back at Arinze; he was leaning back in his chair with his eyes on me. He winked and I smiled before turning back to the field. The next few minutes flew by in a blaze. I watched in awe as the jockeys and their horses did their thing. I had placed a bet on the only Black jockey on the field. I didn't necessarily have any stake in the outcome of the bet, but the experience was worth it. I watched as the highly talked about #19 won. Cheers went up as the winning horse was draped with a garland of roses and the trophy was presented. With my throat hoarse from yelling and my palms sore from clapping, I turned around.

"Baby, d—"

"*Obi m.* I don't have any big speech because no matter what I say here, I guarantee you've heard me say it already. Life's attempt to dim your light brought you to me and I'll forever be grateful. You often credit me for saving you, but every day I get to love, protect, cater, pamper, and pray over you, I'm fulfilled. You give me my reason to smile. In you, my life is whole, and my days have meaning. I'm not easily shaken but the thought of not having that fulfillment for the rest of my days, rattle my core. So, Jasmine Marie Bowman, will you be my wife?"

With my mouth open, tears streamed down my cheeks as I took in what was happening. The love of my life was on one knee, holding the most beautiful princess cut diamond I'd ever seen. I nodded, my eyes quickly darting to Aubree and Cheta who were filming with their phones. My eyes met Arinze's again, who now had one brow lifted.

I nodded between giggles and tears. "Yes, baby. I'd be honored."

Arinze stood and fitted the ring on my finger. He drew me into his arms, and we sealed our engagement with a kiss. I couldn't put into words what I felt so I decided to let my lips speak for me.

GLOSSARY

<u>Pidgin/Igbo/Yoruba Translations</u>

The Kalus are from Enugu State located in the South Eastern part of Nigeria. They're of the Igbo ethnicity. Below are translations (done to the best of my ability) to the languages I used in the story. I have this in the order in which they appear.

Wahala: Problem/Trouble (Pidgin)

Isi Ewu: a traditional Igbo dish that is made with a goat's head.

O we ife ne me gi nisi: Is something wrong with your head or are you crazy?

Ke kwanu: How now or wassup (Igbo)

Asa m! Chai, ne go du! Omalicha nwa: My beauty. Look at you. Beautiful child. (Igbo)

Abeg: Please (Pidgin)

Daalu: Thank You (Igbo)

Omo mi: My child (Yoruba)

O gini di: What is it (Igbo)

Nna mehn: Man (Igbo)

Arrangee: Arrangement (Pidgin)

Check am na: Look at it carefully (Pidgin)

hapụ ihe ahụ: Leave that thing or Don't believe that (Igbo)
Babalawo: Native doctor/Medicine man (Yoruba)
Ndewo: Igbo greeting
Broda : Brother (Pidgin)
Ẹ kú alẹ́: Good evening (Yoruba)
Lati igba wo: Since when (Yoruba)
Obi m : My heart (Igbo)
o zu go: It's enough (Igbo)

FINAL NOTE

Thank you for reading Arinze & Jasmine's story. Please consider leaving a review on the platform you purchased the book. I greatly appreciate honest feedback. They really go a long way. The number of reviews a book receives greatly improves its visibility.

If you liked this story, I trust you might like some of my other titles. But before we get to those, I'd love to stay connected. Never miss a sale, new release announcements, or freebies. Next up in the Kalu family is Cheta Kalu. Order here

You can ensure you're in the know by joining my mailing list.

ALSO BY UNOMA NWANKWOR

Stand Alone Books

An Unexpected Blessing

He Changed My Name

When You Let Go

Full Circle

The Ultimatum Series

The Christmas Ultimatum

The Final Ultimatum

Sons of Ishmael Series

A Scoop of Love

Anchored by Love

Mended with Love

Redeemed Through Love

Mixed Tidings

The Invisible Shackles Series

To Live Again,

To Breathe Again

The DuBois-Arazi Family Novels

A Promise Fulfilled

Destiny Fulfilled

The Billionaire Pact

Vegas Nights

Second Shot

Pretend Bae

Away To Africa

New Year's Kiss (Prequel)

Rent-A-Bae

www.ingramcontent.com/pod-product-compliance
Lightning Source LLC
Chambersburg PA
CBHW021713190726
48289CB00008B/2503